Fright Party

Other books you will enjoy

Ask your bookseller for the books you have missed

THE CASE OF THE DIRTY BIRD, *by Gary Paulsen*

DUNC'S DOLL, *by Gary Paulsen*

CULPEPPER'S CANNON, *by Gary Paulsen*

DUNC GETS TWEAKED, *by Gary Paulsen*

DUNC'S HALLOWEEN, *by Gary Paulsen*

DUNC BREAKS THE RECORD, *by Gary Paulsen*

HOW TO EAT FRIED WORMS, *by Thomas Rockwell*

HOW TO FIGHT A GIRL, *by Thomas Rockwell*

HOW TO GET FABULOUSLY RICH, *by Thomas Rockwell*

EARTH TO MATTHEW, *by Paula Danziger*

EVERYONE ELSE'S PARENTS SAID YES, *by Paula Danziger*

THE WACKY FACTS LUNCH BUNCH

PAUL ZINDEL

Fright Party

Illustrated by
JEFF MANGIAT

A SKYLARK BOOK
NEW YORK • TORONTO • LONDON • SYDNEY • AUCKLAND

RL5, 09-012

FRIGHT PARTY

A Skylark Book / October 1993

Skylark Books is a registered trademark of Bantam Books, a division of Bantam Doubleday Dell Publishing Group, Inc. Registered in U.S. Patent and Trademark Office and elsewhere.

ISBN 0-553-48082-0

Published simultaneously in the United States and Canada

Bantam Books are published by Bantam Books, a division of Bantam Doubleday Dell Publishing Group, Inc. Its trademark, consisting of the words "Bantam Books" and the portrayal of a rooster, is Registered in U.S. Patent and Trademark Office and in other countries. Marca Registrada. Bantam Books, 1540 Broadway, New York, New York 10036.

PRINTED IN THE UNITED STATES OF AMERICA

CWO   0 9 8 7 6 5 4 3 2 1

To Liz, my favorite, fearless,
fantasmagoric daughter

Contents

1 School for Ghouls! 1

2 Fangfurters, Hamboo-gers, and Ice Scream! 11

3 Ghouls and Giggles! 23

4 Skeleton Crew! 35

5 Boning Up! 45

6 Boys and Ghouls, Please Be Sheeted! 53

7 The Abominable Snow Pizza! 63

8 DEMON-stration! 69

9 You Can't Keep a Good Moan Down! 77

10 Raising Spirits! 87

11 Super Natural! 95

12 Ouch! Eeeeeek! Ugh! 115

13 High Spirits! 123

Contents

THE WACKY FACTS LUNCH BUNCH OATH

We, the undersigned, vow to make our fifth grade at New Springville Elementary School cram full of laughs, good times, and mind-boggling adventures—and be the best of friends until death do us part!

Signed in bloodred barbecue sauce,

Dave Martin

_____, PRESIDENT, in charge of *Wacky Facts* and *warp speed action!*

Liz McGinn

_____, EXECUTIVE SECRETARY, specializing in *Knock-Knock jokes, horrifying headlines,* and *secret club notes.*

Johnny Hayes

_____, VICE PRESIDENT, in charge of *Goony Gags, puzzles,* and *"Really Freaky Things to Do"!*

Jennifer Lopez

_____, TREASURER, in charge of *"Ghoulie Foolies," tongue twisters,* and *great money-making ideas!*

MAX MILLNER

_____, OFFICIAL CLUB ARTIST, specializing in *hilarious cartoons* and *excellent funny jokes.*

Fright Party

School for Ghouls!

The Wacky Facts Lunch Bunch snapped to attention the second Mrs. Wilmont asked the class for suggestions on how to celebrate Halloween. I'm not known as Action Dave for nothing. I called out in a flash, "Let's have a Fright Party!" Then I remembered to raise my hand.

Jennifer, Johnny, and Max backed me right up and shouted "Yes!" in agreement.

"Now, exactly what *is* a Fright Party, Dave?" Mrs. Wilmont asked, and I noticed her eyes opened as big as pizzas.

"Everybody thinks up creepy and shocking ways to scare each other! It's a party that's so gross, it's fun!" I said.

"I'm not interested in being scared," Liz moaned.

She twisted her long blond hair like she was going to chew on it. She chews on something whenever she feels nervous.

"Sure, you are! Everybody wants to be scared!" I insisted.

As usual, Johnny, Jennifer, Max, the rest of the WACKY FACTS LUNCH BUNCH, had lots to say. The STUCK-UPS, their faces bored, drummed their fingers. I noticed that the BRAINS kept doing extra-credit work. The SUPERNERDS looked off into space in one direction, and the ZOMBIES in the other. As the JOCKS let out wolfman howls and banged their desks like goofballs, Mrs. Wilmont stood up and called for attention. "Quiet down! Quiet down!" When that didn't work she blew the whistle around her neck.

"WEEEEEEEEEEEEEEEEEEE!"

"A Fright Party sounds like an interesting idea," Mrs. Wilmont said, smiling. "We might be able to learn fascinating things about the history of Halloween."

"Like *what*?" Nat Bronski asked in his usual braying voice. He sounds like a huge, freaked-out moose and I can tell you that's what he looks like, too.

"What's to know about Halloween?" Nat's crony Rado Clapp squeaked up. Nat and Rado belong to their own group of *two*. Everyone calls them the

NASTY BLOBS behind their backs. They are two of the most rotten, nutty goons in the whole school.

"Do you know who started Halloween?" Mrs. Wilmont asked, walking around the room as she spoke.

"I know," Liz said, "the Druids. They are the people who built Stonehenge."

"How did you know that?" Mrs. Wilmont seemed impressed.

"Dave told me," Liz answered. She always gives me credit, which is one more reason I like her. "Dave knows lots of shocking facts!"

Mrs. Wilmont pulled on her left ear almost as if she was petting her panda earring. Mrs. Wilmont wears jewelry that is connected to Endangered Species. I think she likes animals as much as kids.

"What other interesting facts can you share with us, Dave?" she asked.

"I've read that in the Middle Ages people in Europe reported seeing cats turn into vicious elves, mean goblins, and bloodthirsty witches. On Halloween people made bonfires to ward off the evil spirits!"

"What you're telling us is correct," Mrs. Wilmont said. "It's amazing what strange things people from other times have believed. Does anyone know anything else about Halloween?"

Jimmy Quinn, one of the Brains, raised his

hand. "Halloween got its name from being known as 'All Hallows Eve,' " he said. "I read about the history in an encyclopedia. The Celts came after the Druids. They had festivals for two gods. One was a sun god. The other was a god of the dead."

"Excellent, Jimmy," Mrs. Wilmont said.

"I still think we should have a Fright Party," I reminded everyone.

"It's too *dumb*," Nat sneered.

"Why do you think a Fright Party is dumb, Nat?" Mrs. Wilmont turned to him.

"Nothing ever scares me!" Nat said, and added a burp.

"*We* could scare you *easy*," I said loudly. Nat knew I was talking about me and the Wacky Facts Lunch Bunch.

"Not in a zillion years!" Nat snapped.

"Yes, we can!" Liz, Johnny, Jennifer, and Max chanted almost as if they'd rehearsed it. The first week in fifth grade we'd stuck together like glue when it came to dealing with the Nasty Blobs, and we'd beat them.

"Do you have a better idea?" Mrs. Wilmont asked Nat.

"Yeah," Nat said. "Why don't we have a frog cook-off? We could all bring in live frogs, and cook them!"

"Yeah." Rado giggled. "Or we could poach them

or stir-fry them. How do you like to cook *your* frogs, Mrs. Wilmont?"

"I wouldn't put one in a microwave, if I were you," Nat howled. "They explode!"

"Nat and Rado *did* that once," one of the Nerds called out.

Mrs. Wilmont stopped in front of Nat's and Rado's desks. I thought they looked spooked. I knew she wouldn't smack them, but I was surprised when she said, "The more you two tell me, the better a Fright Party sounds. But I want the whole class to think about what to do, and we'll pool our ideas tomorrow. We have five days before Halloween."

"Booooooooooring!" Nat belched again. "Nothing will ever scare *me*."

"As you know," Mrs. Wilmont said, "every year each class decorates its room for Halloween. We are going to do something *special*."

"What?" we all wanted to know.

She held up a coin that looked like an old quarter. "This is a very old coin. I bought it last summer when I was visiting my sister who lives in England. It caught my eye when she took me to a flea market in a small town near the ancient ruins of Stonehenge."

"Can I hold it?" Liz was close to Mrs. Wilmont and asked without even raising her hand.

"Of course," Mrs. Wilmont said, handing it to

her. "Take a look, then pass it around for everyone to see. I wanted a souvenir from my visit to a place filled with legends and folklore, so I bought the coin. Many people think Stonehenge is magical. This coin is not very valuable. I guess I hoped it would be a talisman."

"What's a *talisman*?" Johnny asked.

"It's another word for a **charm**," Mrs. Wilmont explained. "I wanted it to protect me from harm and bring me good fortune."

"Did it work?" Max asked, reaching to take the coin from Liz. Liz held on to it as if she didn't want to give up the coin. Finally, she handed it to Max.

"Of course, it brought me the good fortune of having you for a class!" Mrs. Wilmont laughed. I think she really meant it. "When I came across it this morning I thought how much I'd really like to give it to one of *you* to keep! It's important to pass along good fortune, although we usually are involved in making our own."

Even the Zombies woke up when Mrs. Wilmont announced that someone would get to keep the coin.

"You're kidding," Jennifer said.

"What do we have to do for it?" Nat sneered.

"I want each of you to come up with your own talisman. I want you to ***invent*** your own lucky charm." Mrs. Wilmont smiled. "Make a lucky symbol out of clay or wood or papier-mâché, anything.

You can make it as big as you want, and in any shape to protect you from your worst nightmare! And give it a name of some sort so we know exactly what kind of charm it is!"

"But I love nightmares!" Nat called out.

"Fine," Mrs. Wilmont said. "You can make a charm in the shape of a demon or a monster. A devilish charm ought to attract all the nightmares anyone could want!"

"Great!" Nat managed to say in a human voice. I didn't even think he was capable of that.

"Use your imaginations and come up with whatever you like," Mrs. Wilmont urged. "I will be the judge. Whoever makes the most creative talisman will win my lucky coin. It'll be a contest! No grade on this project. Just the pleasure of creating something—and maybe winning the lucky coin."

"What'll happen to the losers?" Jennifer asked, tossing her long, black ponytail behind her.

"There won't be any losers," Mrs. Wilmont explained. "We'll put everyone's talisman on display. We'll invite other classes to see them. I want us to have the best decorations in the school!"

A Brain in front passed the coin to me. It was yellowish-brown, almost rusty. On one side I could make out the face of a cranky guy—I guess an emperor—with a two-headed snake on his shoulder. When I turned the coin over, **I noticed secret-looking, mysterious words on it.**

Liz reached her hand across the aisle to me and asked, "Can I hold it again?"

"Sure," I said. "I think everyone's had a look."

She took the coin back and stared at it. *How could I possibly have figured right there and then that she'd go bonkers if she didn't win Mrs. Wilmont's magical coin!*

Fangfurters, Hamboo-gers, and Ice Scream!

The bell rang and we all headed down for lunch. On the stairs, Liz's one-track mind kept going on about Mrs. Wilmont's magic coin. "I'll never win it, but I need her luck!"

"Don't get so worked up," I told her. "It's really only an old coin. If it were a shark's tooth the Solomon Island natives used to use for money, I'd be interested."

"What kind of charm are you going to make?" Liz asked all of us.

"I don't know," Jennifer answered first.

"Me, either," Johnny echoed.

"A charm is something you can't talk about too much or it'll lose its power." Max looked very serious.

"I'm going to make a charm to protect me

against too much homework," I announced. **"Maybe it'll be a voodoo doll with the head of a ghoul."**

"I really don't even like the idea of making anything that has to do with monsters," Liz complained. "I don't want to touch, see, or think about anything crawly."

"Maybe that's why you always get sick on Halloween," Johnny reasoned.

"I do not always get sick," Liz replied defensively.

"Yes, you do," Jennifer said. "I think the longest you've ever gone out for **TRICK OR TREATING** with us is maybe twenty minutes and then you go home!"

"So what if I just don't like Halloween," Liz protested. "Is that so weird?"

"All kids like Halloween," Max said. "What kid doesn't like ringing doorbells, wearing a wacky costume, and getting free candy?"

"See? That's just what Halloween is—one big beggars' holiday," Liz said. "I don't see anything so great about kids going begging all over the neighborhood. I'd rather just ask my mom for five bucks and buy the candy I want!"

"Well, I love monsters," I said, "and Halloween ranks as my second-favorite holiday. My favorite is my birthday, I think."

"My mom said if you think about monsters

too much, they'll come after you," Jennifer warned.

"Halloween is one thing. Monsters are another." Liz groaned. "I don't want to worry about either. I'm worried about winning the magic coin!"

The cafeteria was a madhouse as usual. Kids ran around like chickens with their heads chopped off, blabbing a mile a minute and stuffing food into their faces. The reason we had formed our club in the lunchroom was because we wanted to be officially organized and connected. The kids all split up into the same groups they do in class—the Stuckups, the Brains, the Supernerds, the Zombies, and the Jocks have their own tables. Even the Nasty Blobs. So we formed our club the very first day of fifth grade. We staked out our own table. We have the best one, near the windows and farthest away from the steam table—which always has at least one special that smells like **boiled mongoose** and looks like **baked mouse.**

"I officially call the Wacky Facts Lunch Bunch to order," I announced. "We have a lot of stuff to go over today, so we'd better get moving!"

"I brought in a **Ghoulie Foolie,**" Jennifer said, stabbing at her noodle salad. It wiggled like fat, juicy, disgusting white worms. She's a health-food nut and always eats something weird and yucky.

"Great," Max said, a gooey piece of pizza cheese hanging off his chin.

"What's worse than a werewolf who has to get a rabies shot?" Jennifer asked between noodle bites.

"I don't know." Johnny was straight man.

"A vampire who needs braces!" Jennifer giggled and so did Liz and Max.

"Ghoulies are great," I said, "but wait until you hear this new **Wacky Fact.** *A kid from New Jersey tried to sell his mother to pirates for a new CD player!"*

Nobody believed me but I swore it was true. I started collecting Wacky Facts in the third grade, and now, anytime I see or hear a weird fact, I add it to the club files. Liz, Johnny, Jennifer, and Max love my Wacky Facts, too, but they have other specialties. Our club also has a collection of gags, puzzles, and cartoons that is really mind-boggling!

"Knock-Knock," Liz said. She never tires of **KK's,** her favorite kind of joke.

"Who's there?" I played the straight guy this time.

"Boo hoo," she said.

"Boo hoo *who*?" I asked.

"Boo hoo hoo **hoo,**" she said.

I thought she was going bonkers. *"Boo hoo hoo who?"*

"Stop crying," Liz said, laughing. "You're breaking my heart!"

Jennifer rolled her eyes and grunted. "I heard

that joke three hundred twenty-seven times before. It's so corny I could really upchuck this second!"

"Like your joke was so original!" Liz was searching for a straw for her chocolate milk, but smiled a *just-kidding* smile at Jennifer. Liz and I usually always buy the cafeteria lunch. Max, who only has his dad, buys his lunch, too. Jennifer's mom and dad own a grocery store so she's always eating healthy foods like squash and stuff that looks like hay. Johnny's mother always packs him a lip-smacking lunch. When it comes to eating, he's Johnny-on-the-spot, but he never gets fat.

Johnny pulled out his gag for the day. "I made a **PENCIL THROUGH YOUR HEAD,**" Johnny said, munching on a meat-loaf sandwich dripping with gravy. It was a strip of metal from an old pair of earmuffs. He'd glued the eraser half of a pencil to one end, and the writing-point half to the other end. When he put it on it did look as if the pencil were going through his head like an arrow.

"That's horrible," Liz said.

"Hey, it's a riot," I said.

"You can make smaller ones, too," Johnny said, laughing. "Then you can have PENCIL THROUGH YOUR ARM and **PENCIL THROUGH YOUR NOSE.** When I showed it to my mom last night, she almost passed out."

Max handed around a cartoon he'd drawn. "I did **TALKING PUMPKINS,**" he said.

Johnny, Jennifer, and I chuckled, but I saw that although Liz tried to laugh, her mind was elsewhere. I didn't think she was worrying about how she was going to win Mrs. Wilmont's magic coin.

"I saved my very best Wacky Fact for last. It's going to blow your socks off," I warned.

Jennifer groaned. "My socks stayed on the last time you said that. Remember your fact about the French farmer who made his donkeys wear underpants?"

"This is a really important fact," I said, and then leaned in closer and whispered so nobody at any other table could hear. "It's got to do with the Fright Party. It's so great I'm almost going to explode!"

"What is it?" Johnny whispered back.

"Last night I came across the spookiest fact in the world," I explained. "It's about Houdini."

"Who's *Houdini*?" Jennifer asked.

"You don't know who Houdini is?" Johnny gasped. **"He's only the greatest magician that ever lived, that's all!"**

"Big deal. He's not even on TV," Jennifer said. "At least I've never seen him."

"Me, either," Liz agreed with Jennifer for a change.

"Of course not! Because he's *dead*!" I said, trying not to lose my patience. "Houdini died in Detroit, Michigan, in 1926."

"That's not a very nice *Wacky* Fact." Liz shook

her head disapprovingly. "A dead magician who's never been on TV? Come on, Dave!"

"Wait," I said, "but if I told you he died on *Halloween* in 1926, that's a different story, isn't it? **And if I added that he promised to come back from the grave, and if you knew he even had a telephone buried in his coffin with him so he could make the call—that's *interesting*, isn't it! That's a Wacky Fact and spooky, too—well, isn't it?"**

"You're giving me chills, Dave Martin." Liz shivered and chewed her left little finger. "Why are you telling us this?"

"I want us to throw the most horrifying Fright Party any fifth grade class has ever seen!" I admitted. "And I want it to be so frightening the Blobs will freak out."

"I agree with Dave. I'd like to see Nat really toss his cookies," Johnny said, and Max laughed.

"And that Rado is really such a rodent," Jennifer chimed in.

"Exactly." I smiled because everyone agreed with me. "That's why we've all got to start thinking of the scariest things we can!"

"Let's do it!" Max urged, and this time Johnny nodded.

"Maybe the Fright Party should be bigger than just our class. Maybe it should be for all three fifth grade classes," Max suggested. "There's a meeting of the Student Council after school today. Since you guys helped get me elected Class Rep, I could bring it up for a vote."

"Great idea," Jennifer said.

Liz, who looked like she had indigestion, finally spoke up. "Why don't you just have a Fright Party on Halloween for the whole cafeteria?"

"Hey, that's even a better idea," I said. I really meant it, but Liz looked ready to kick me. **"Why stop there?" she yelled. "Make it one big Fright Party for the whole school. Or the *whole world!*"**

"For someone who hates Halloween," I said to Liz, "you're thinking of one great Fright Party!"

"I was just joking," Liz protested, but now Jennifer was cutting her off.

"I know how to make a great bowl of eyeballs," Jennifer bragged.

"What are you talking about?" Johnny asked.

"Well," Jennifer replied, "I went to a party once and here's what they did. Before the party they put grapes in a pan and covered them with slimy egg whites, so that when we touched them in a dark room they felt just like *eyeballs.*"

Liz scrunched up her face.

"My mother makes homemade noodles. When they're raw, I tease my brothers because the noodles are so slippery. I could put them in a bowl and we could say they were *vampire brains*," Johnny suggested.

"Great," I said.

"Great?" Liz yelled in disbelief. "It's disgusting."

"That's the point," Johnny said, smiling.

"Terrific," I said. "The secret is having everyone in the dark! We need *dark*! We've got to make sure wherever we have the party we can pull the shades."

"How about *here*? Look around. This cafeteria's got great shades," Johnny said.

He was right. Half the time classes double up and have to see movies in the lunchroom.

"Maybe each table could try to scare the other ones if they wanted!" I practically shouted.

"You're making it sound like a fright *contest*!" Liz twitched.

"That's it!" Johnny whooped. We were making so much noise the Supernerds at the next table stared at us.

"And I know the theme for our table!" I roared.

"What?" Liz asked, looking ready to sock me.

"Nightmare Alley!" I sneered as if I were evil. *"We'll make our table into a super, horrifying, and bloodcurdling Nightmare Alley! It'll be ghastly and really gross. AND I MEAN GROSS! And we'll GET Nat the Blob! Rado's already a mouse! It's Nat Bronski we've got to scare to death!"*

THREE

Ghouls and Giggles!

After school I went home. I always try to remember to enter my house with my right foot first because I came across the Wacky Fact that the ancient Romans believed the left side of the body attracts evil. **In fact, the Latin word for left is "sinister," and with Halloween coming up I didn't want to mess with Fate.**

I let our Great Dane, **Darwin,** out into the backyard, and did my homework. I wanted the whole evening free to think of awful things for the Fright Party and our Nightmare Alley that would really terrify the Nasty Blobs. The only distraction I had was from my eight-year-old sister who asks questions and laughs all the time. Her real name is Gillian. When she was five years old one of our baby-sitters called her *Giggles.* The nickname stuck for good reasons. Giggles is the only person who calls me *Davie*, which I can't stand. I'm not a *Davie*, I'm a **Dave**.

"*Davie*, does God make lamb chops?" This question was her excuse to come into my room. She asks me that question twenty-five times a year ever since she watched a TV documentary on Australian sheep farming. I think my parents let her watch too many PBS and educational programs.

"No, Giggles," I said. "*People* make lamb chops."

"From *what*?"

"From *wool*," I told her, but she knew I was kidding. She laughed for ten minutes over that one. Once I told her they made lamb chops out of plastic.

Giggles is in the second grade at my school. Somehow she always manages to get a hall pass and she tracks me down. The last time she caught up with me at lunch she told me she heard a really great joke about a rooster who was afraid to fight because he was chicken. She loves to copy everything I do and sometimes it really gets on my nerves. Another time in the middle of an all-school assembly she saw me and yelled out, "That's my brother! That's my brother, *Davie*! *Hi, Davie! Hi, Davie!*"

Mom came in at five thirty. She works in the Classified Ad Department at the *New Springville Tribune*. I went down and helped cut up some string beans and put them in the steamer along with some peas. Mom concentrated on getting an egg dip ready for veal cutlets.

"There's an article I think you'll like in tonight's paper," she said, as she breaded the cutlets.

"What's it about?"

"Rodents," she answered, "how they can eat through cement walls, and go without water longer than camels. I hate talking about rodents while I'm making dinner, but it's the wacky stuff you like."

"Great. Thanks, Mom," I said.

"What's the scariest thing that ever happened to you?" I asked her. Then I told her all about the upcoming Fright Party.

"That's easy," she said, flipping the cutlets over. "I remember spending a summer in the mountains when I was about your age. One foggy morning I was walking along the road when I thought I saw a car heading for me."

"What happened?"

"Well, when it got closer, I could see it was a *bear*!"

"What did you do?"

"Luckily, my grandfather came along in a truck, looking for me because I wasn't supposed to be out alone. We ended up frightening the bear as much as the bear frightened me!"

When my father came home a half hour later, he began to make the salad. He adds blue cheese and walnuts, and looks so involved it's like he's making an atomic bomb.

When we sat down at the table to eat, I told him all about my idea for NIGHTMARE ALLEY. "Dad, do you have any good fright suggestions?"

"Tell a *suggestion*, Daddy. Tell us one," Giggles said, laughing. She always sticks her two cents in.

My father patted Giggles on her head as if she were the dog. "I remember there was one Halloween party I went to as a kid that really scared me," he said.

"What scared you, Daddy? What?" Giggles was talking with her mouth full. She started to really get on my nerves.

"Don't eat with your fingers!" Mom reminded her.

"This kid Larry really wanted to scare everyone," Dad went on, "so he dimmed the lights. Suddenly, we all saw a mummy. He'd wrapped himself up in toilet paper, and made sounds to scare us."

"The boy wrapped himself in toilet paper?" Giggles repeated, wide-eyed. *"Toilet paper?"*

"Yep."

"That doesn't sound very scary," Mom said. "Dave's looking for something grisly."

"Don't rush the story." Dad looked at Mom. "Some of the kids were scared by the toilet-paper mummy, but I wasn't. What scared me was the *mummy's handshake!*"

I was interested to hear what my father had to say, but Giggles was wiggling in her chair.

"*Jack,*" Mom scolded my dad, "you're upsetting Giggles."

"No," Giggles corrected, using her knife like a hockey stick to sock around the peas on her plate. "Mummies are nice. Very nice. I want Daddy to go on."

"What was so scary about the mummy's hand-shake?" I wanted to know.

"Well," Dad explained, "the mummy reached out to shake my hand, and when I touched it, its hand felt scaly and slimy as if it really had come from a damp tomb. I remember even now how it sent chills through my whole body."

"What was it, *really*?" I asked, sitting on the edge of my seat.

"Okay, I'll tell you, although it took us a week to persuade Tim to tell us! He wore a pair of rubber dishwashing gloves, and he had put a lot of olive oil and talcum powder on them," Dad explained. "They came out greasy and cakey and scaly and really felt horrible, and very, very real!"

"I want to be a toilet-paper mummy for Hallow-een this year!" Giggles squealed like a police siren. "*I want to be a toilet-paper mummy!*"

"Fine with me," Mom said. "It'll be a lot cheaper than buying a costume in a store. Just please stop smacking your peas!"

After dinner, Max called me. "Everybody's very excited about having a Fright Party," he explained, and gave me details of what happened at the Student Council meeting.

"Can we use the lunchroom?"

"I think so," Max said. "Mr. Donahue, the faculty advisor, thought it'd be a great idea as long as none of the first and second graders were around. He said he'd discuss it with the principal and teachers involved."

"Way to go!" I cheered. Then I told him about the *mummy's handshake,* and asked him if he'd come up with any other scary ideas.

"I was thinking we could make our lunch table into a *really* dark NIGHTMARE ALLEY," Max said.

"How?"

"We could stretch a heavy cord from one of the doorways to the metal mesh on the windows," he explained. "Then we could hang sheets and blankets over it so it'd be **extra** dark!"

"It'd be like an actual alley!"

"Yes."

"Now we're cooking! We are *cooking*!" I yelled. "Kids could just file through like they were going into a crypt. We'd have a much better chance to really spook them!"

When Jennifer called she had an eyeball report. There were three different kinds of juicy grapes in her parents' store, and she and her mom would test them after dinner with egg gook on them.

"Red Globe grapes are nice and big and round and each one *looks* like a Cyclops' eyeball," she was happy to say. "I think they're going to be fabulously gross."

"Make sure you find the right amount of slime for them."

"No problem."

"Dave, I'm really glad you called," Liz said when I called her. "I was just going to call you!"

"It's ESP. I felt your brain waves," I kidded.

"You *didn't*!"

"You're right. I *didn't*," I said, laughing.

"Look," she said, "I know this will sound crazy, but I just have it in my head that if I win the magic coin, it'll protect me from a certain fear I have."

"Yes, go on," I said.

"What do you mean?" she asked.

"Does this have something to do with why you don't like Halloween?"

"Yes," she answered weakly.

"What are you afraid of?"

"I don't want to tell you because you'll laugh."

"I won't laugh."

"And do you promise you won't tell another soul about it? Not even another member of the Wacky Facts Lunch Bunch?" Liz sounded very serious.

"I promise," I said. *"I promise."*

"Well, if you must know," she said, **"I'm afraid a terrible, horrible beast is going to come after me and—"**

I couldn't control my voice and I howled.

"You promised you wouldn't laugh, and you did!" Liz yelled.

"I'm sorry," I apologized quickly. "What kind of a beast do you think is going to come get you?"

"It sounds stupid and silly, but it's an ugly creature with fur, and claws—and the most terrifying thing is, its head seems like a dead man's, and the other half is a shriveled lizard's. I see this frightening mouth, with huge, yellow needle teeth and awful juices drip from it. I've had this nightmare a lot. It wants me for *food*." Her voice shuddered.

"How long have you dreamed about this thing?"

"Ever since I stayed up and watched a whole night of horror videos with my older brother."

"What did you watch?"

"*Alien, King Kong,* and *Night of the Living Dead*—and MORE! I was only in the first grade," she admitted.

"That was *four* years ago!"

"So? I was six years old and saw all those apes and mutations and creepy people climbing up out of graves and taking over a whole town. I can't stop those images. Well, they stopped for a while, but every Halloween they come back. I just think if I had Mrs. Wilmont's magic coin I wouldn't be afraid anymore—and maybe I wouldn't feel so weird about Halloween."

Liz and I've been friends since we were little kids. I knew about her regular anxiety that made her eat popcorn. Practically every day she's worried about helping somebody with a problem or saving the ozone layer. She says the world is going so crazy it makes her stomach growl, which is why she wants to chew on something to quiet it down.

Her older brother Pete is her stepbrother, who's away at college. Liz reads all his psychology books. She ate four bags of popcorn one night when she read a case study about a Winnipeg dentist who thought he was a toad.

"Tonight I did something awful all because you had to open your big mouth about Houdini being buried with a phone," Liz complained.

"What?"

"I read one of my brother's books on the subject of GHOSTS!"

"So, what'd you find out?"

"Revolting things."

"Like what?"

"Like there are two kinds," she groaned. "*Mean* ones that come back just to GET you. They're the worst kind."

"What about *good* ghosts?" I asked. "Houdini's

ghost is probably a really nice kind of guy. Too bad he didn't die more recently because it'd be easier for him to make a phone call."

"What are you talking about?"

"I heard a news item about an undertakers' convention that said bodies don't decay very fast anymore because everyone's food nowadays has a lot more preservatives in it."

"Enough with the Wacky Facts, Dave," Liz ordered. **"All this book said was that with good ghosts, *you* have to be the one trying to reach them. That's the only reason they come back— because you ask them to."**

Suddenly, an idea hit me so hard I couldn't speak. That happens a lot when a real slam-dunk idea grabs me! I can't talk. I don't even know I'm not talking.

"Dave, are you still there?" Liz's voice came over the phone. "Dave, did you just think of something crazy? Did you?" Liz and I have been pals so long she knows me better than I know myself. *"Dave, what are you thinking?"*

"I just realized how we can really scare the Nasty Blobs," I said, and I meant it.

"How?" she asked, sounding curious in spite of herself.

"It'll be the climax of our Fright Party! It'll be fantastic! We'll do something that'll make those Blobs really shake, rattle, and croak."

"What?"

"We'll call up the ghost of Houdini!" I shouted. "We'll get Houdini's ghost to return right in the cafeteria! Right in front of everyone! Especially Nat Bronski!" I squealed with delight. *"We'll call Houdini back from the dead!"*

Skeleton Crew!

As usual, the next morning all of us in the Wacky Facts Lunch Bunch got to school a half hour early to work on Mrs. Wilmont's lab squad. She's in charge of all the science equipment for the school, and gives us service credits each term for helping. We volunteered at the beginning of the term because we figured we could also use the time for our club members to be together.

"Good morning!" Mrs. Wilmont sang cheerfully at the sight of us. "You all look bright and bushy-tailed this morning!"

It didn't seem the right time to tell her about our plan to contact Houdini at the Fright Party.

"Morning, Mrs. Wilmont," we said. Liz and Jennifer complimented her on her rhinoceros earrings and necklace. I was more interested in the Fright Party.

"Here are all the teachers' order slips for today." Mrs. Wilmont handed them to us. "I have a faculty meeting about scheduling the Halloween parties. By now I'm sure you can handle these deliveries yourselves. Are you comfortable with that?"

"Yes, Mrs. Wilmont," we said, like a chorus.

"We'd really like to have the Fright Party in the cafeteria," I added.

"You mentioned that yesterday, Dave. I won't forget," she promised.

The minute she left, the idea crossed my mind that practically all the thingamajigs we had to deliver that morning was stuff that'd be great to borrow for the Fright Party.

"Mrs. Carter in Room 201 wants the skeleton," I said. "Wouldn't it be great for our Nightmare Alley?"

"Maybe we could put it in a dress," Jennifer suggested.

"Yeah," Johnny agreed. "And a hat."

Max read another one of the order slips. "Mr. Fisler wants the preserved eels in a jar. That'd scare a lot of people if we stuck a flashlight right below them so they made shadows on a sheet!"

"We could shake them a little so they *move!*" Johnny added.

"Terrific," I said. ***"Zombie eels!"***

Liz grunted and picked out the order she wanted. "I'll bring Mr. Breiden the giant plastic model of the flower. At least that's not gross."

"No, but it *could* be," Johnny said, perking up.

"How?" I wanted to know.

"We could make a couple of extra-big leaves out of foam rubber, and one of us could stand behind it and try to eat kids as they went by," he explained. "It'd be really good in the dark."

"We could make it into a gooey Venus's-flytrap!" Jennifer agreed.

"Cool," I said.

"Oh, yuck and double yuck," Liz complained.

"Just think what we could do with the preserved pig and squid!" I said.

"Mrs. DiGuiseppi wants the static electricity machine," Johnny read from a slip. "I bet I could rig up something so that when anyone sat in a special chair they'd get a good shock."

"Too dangerous," I said. "Mrs. Wilmont wouldn't like it. She'd never let us."

"Dave's right," Jennifer admitted.

"Just deliver the stuff, will you?" Liz said, grabbing the big plastic flower and heading out the door.

By the time Mrs. Wilmont came back from her meeting, we had finished all the deliveries and it wasn't even time for class to begin.

"Well," Mrs. Wilmont announced, "thanks to Max and the Student Council, you've got the cafeteria for the Fright Party."

We cheered and I gave Max a high five. "Can we run down to the cafeteria for a few minutes before class?" I asked Mrs. Wilmont.

"Sure," Mrs. Wilmont agreed. "Volunteering pays off!"

In a flash we were down the stairs and in the empty cafeteria. We'd never looked at the lunchroom in terms of a Halloween party before.

"I think the lunch tables look like grave plots!" Jennifer pointed out.

"Ugh," Liz grunted. "Don't say that."

"We can get a clothesline across here easily," Johnny said as he checked out the window and doorway near our table. "We'll be able to hang the sheets and blankets on it."

"It's going to make a great Nightmare Alley," Max agreed.

"You know, my *eyeballs* aren't going to *feel* like eyeballs, unless we put the idea in everybody's heads," Jennifer said.

"Yeah," Johnny agreed. "We've got to influence everyone—if they know what to expect, their imaginations will run wild."

"We need a few ads—is that what you're saying?" I asked.

"We've got to get kids in the mood and then it will be easier to feel frightened," Max agreed.

"Right on," Johnny said. "We can do neat stuff like posters of bats and skulls and hanging fake rats."

"Liz, you could tell fortunes by using **Tarot** cards," Jennifer suggested.

"Are you out of your mind?" Liz demanded.

I hoped Liz might tell the others about her secret fear of being eaten by a horrible beast—but she kept quiet so I did, too, of course.

"Liz could sit in a gypsy costume at the entrance to our Nightmare Alley," Jennifer went on, "and each kid could have his or her fortune told before going down the alley."

"What would Liz say?" Johnny asked.

Jennifer cackled, and imitating a witch, she began, "Something horrible is going to happen to you. Something wicked and chilling. Evil spirits are after you!"

"Why *me*?" Liz protested, and I certainly knew why. "Jennifer can be the fortune-teller. She thought this up!"

"But you're the best actress," Jennifer insisted. "You always get picked for the big parts in school plays."

"You've got to do *something*," Max said.

"All right, I'll tell fortunes," Liz agreed, rolling

her eyes at me. "But I'm not going to tell anyone that a werewolf's waiting to bite their neck or a vampire's going to grab their leg."

"Speaking of the devil," Jennifer groaned. Nat and Rado had strolled into the lunchroom. Anytime they stroll anywhere it's trouble. They saw us.

"Hey, what's new, wackos?" Nat called to us.

"Congratulations," Johnny called back to them.

"On what?" Rado bit.

"We heard your mothers finally got termite insurance on your heads!" Johnny said.

We all laughed.

They flicked us off and headed toward the cooks who were still setting up for the day. The chief dietician, Mrs. Rowan, was cleaning up the front of the steam table to get it ready to hold the hot specials, while a couple of the other cafeteria ladies were making sandwiches and chopping lettuce. Mrs. Rowan is a nice lady with white hair. She treats all the kids like she's their grandmother.

"Hey, Mrs. Rowan, you got any chocolate milk?" Nat asked. His whole big mouth is shaped like a bullhorn so you can hear him a mile away.

"The delivery's late today," Mrs. Rowan apologized. "Sorry, boys, or I'd give you some."

"That's okay," Nat said, taking a napkin. Rado did the same.

"You're really busy today, aren't you, Mrs. Rowan?" Rado squeaked.

"As a matter of fact, I am," she said, smiling, as she bent back down to clean the sides of the steam table. She no sooner lowered her head than Nat and Rado tore pieces of napkins and dropped them onto Mrs. Rowan's head.

Quickly, Jennifer slapped a book on the lunch table to make a loud noise. Mrs. Rowan looked up fast and caught the Blobs sprinkling paper into her hair. She's used to having lots of tricks pulled on her.

"Stop sticking paper in my hair." Mrs. Rowan glared at the Blobs.

"No, we're not!" Nat told her. "It's *snowing*!"

"Or else you've got really big dandruff!" Rado giggled.

The Nasty Blobs laughed out loud, then turned and marched over to us. They were obviously furious that the noise of Jennifer's book hitting the table made them get caught. "You're all a pack of squealers, you know," Nat growled. "A pack of wimps, goody-goodies, and squealers!"

"We'll see who's a wimp Friday at the Fright Party," I said.

"Who are you kidding? You losers couldn't scare diddily!" Nat blurted.

"Yeah," Rado said.

I looked Nat straight in his bloodshot eyes. "We'll scare *you*! We've got something waiting for you that's going to make your blood run cold." I lowered my voice so deep I made a spooky wheezing sound that almost scared me.

Nat's mouth dropped open. He's the only bully I know who's so dumb that when his brain runs out of nasty words and he can't win an argument, he lets out an idiotic wolf howl.

"HOOOOOOOWWLLLLLLLLLLLLLLLLL!"

"Those Nasty Blobs really make me mad," Liz said, tapping her foot as the two walked away.

My mind was spinning on to something important. Something that made me smile—something we could really use for the party.

I pointed.

"What?" Liz asked.

"The steam table," I said.

"What about the steam table?" Liz asked suspiciously. It was empty. Under its four red heat lights, vapors of steam began to wiggle upward.

"This thing will be our silver *altar*!" I said.

"What are you talking about?" Max asked.

"I mean, it's a great place to have scary things happen!" I explained. "The ancient guys who built Stonehenge always had an altar where all the important things would happen. That's where they'd have all their sacrifices!"

Liz scrunched up her nose. "That steam table is no sacrifice altar."

"Sure, it is." Johnny jumped in. "Think of all the fish that have bit the dust there. All the fillets of sole!"

"And the fried chickens," Jennifer said.

"And the boiled mongooses." Max laughed.

"Yes! Yes! Yes!" I raced over to the shiny aluminum steam table with the rest of the Wacky Facts Lunch Bunch right behind me. "I read in *SUPER WEIRD NEWS* that a great Roman poet by the name of Virgil once sacrificed a fly and held a funeral for it so he could tax-exempt his home as a burial ground!"

"That's really and truly loony," Liz complained.

Mrs. Rowan looked up curiously from the vapors. Under the lights she looked like a friendly, puzzled witch.

"Here at this altar," I vowed, smacking the **steam table,** "it will happen. *Here's where we're going to make Nat Bronski meet the ghost of Houdini!"*

Boning Up!

By the afternoon art period, everyone in class was working on the project to make their charms and talismans. Art materials were available for us in the art supply closet. The only rule was we should use what we needed, but put the rest back.

"Can I hold the Stonehenge coin again?" Liz asked.

"Of course," Mrs. Wilmont said as she was busily working on the aquarium. "The coin is in the top left-hand drawer of my desk."

Our classroom has the best aquarium in the school. Mrs. Wilmont selected snails, a catfish, and seven small white fish who keep swimming to the top and it looked like they were kissing each other. I saw that Mrs. Wilmont had a bunch of Day-Glo orange grinning jack-o'-lantern stickers pasted on the back of the aquarium. Even in daylight it looked like the pumpkins were staring out from under the water. It was a riot. Mrs. Wilmot was obviously really into Halloween. I noticed that she had on pumpkin earrings.

I was walking to the front of the room to get supplies. Kids were grabbing stuff. I dipped my hands deep into the gooky clay tin next to Mrs. Wilmot's desk. Liz was opening the top drawer and found the coin. The face of the cranky emperor looked up at us. Liz took the coin and went back to her seat.

I took a piece of oilcloth and a fat clump of clay to my desk, which is right next to Liz's. I really like smacking clay around and sticking my fingers in it to make oozing noises. **At one point I looked up and in the classroom doorway I saw a face grinning and waving at me from the hall. It was my sister, Giggles, who didn't seem to want anything. She was just out on a pass to make faces at me. I waved back, and then ignored her until she went away.**

"Hey, Dave, what kind of a charm are you making?" Johnny asked.

"I decided on a skull," I said. "I need protection against too much homework. I want to make the skull so ugly it'll keep homework away for a year. What're you making?"

"A 3-D paper hamburger with the face of Freddy Krueger." Johnny laughed as he cut out a big oval shape from a piece of white oak tag. "This is going to be the onion slice!"

"What kind of stupid charm is that?" Jennifer asked.

"It's my **GREAT PROTECTOR OF JUNK FOOD**," Johnny said. "See, no matter how much you or my mother nag me, this charm will protect my right to eat all the Cheez Doodles and Gummi Bears I want!"

"You're nuts!" Jennifer laughed. "I was thinking of making a papier-mâché lettuce. Maybe I could put radishes in it for eyes and a turnip for a nose. I want it to ward off cholesterol."

"I don't know exactly what I'm going to make, but I think it's going to be some kind of a friendship charm," Max said.

The talismans the Wacky Facts Lunch Bunch were making weren't the weirdest in the class. Tommy Russo, a Supernerd, was working on a huge crepe-paper pizza charm. Jimmy Quinn, one of the Brains, was making a big, shiny worm out of silver foil. The Jocks were all making monster charms shaped like baseballs, footballs, and basketballs. They said they were going to protect their home runs, touchdowns, and slam dunks. A lot of other kids were into the usual stuff like pig faces, bats, skeletons, spiders, witches, and goggle glasses.

As Liz stared at the coin in her hands, she let out a deep sigh. "I'm never going to come up with anything to win," she said.

"Don't worry about it," I reminded her. "It's how you play the game that counts, not just winning."

She shot me a grumpy look, then got up and put the coin back in Mrs. Wilmont's desk. She took a piece of oilcloth for her own desk and sat back down with a big fat lump of wet clay. She smacked it around until it looked like a volcano. *"I just don't like monsters or scary things. This assignment stinks!"*

After a while the class got so noisy that Mrs. Wilmont took her whistle in her right hand and blew. "WEEEEEEEE!" Her left hand clutched three fat snails and a tangle of dripping water plants. "We're making too much noise," she said, frowning, "but are we having fun?"

The whole class whooped.

Mrs. Wilmont put the plants and snails back into the aquarium. She headed for the blackboard. "Now that most of us have gotten a good start on our charms, I think we should take a moment to consider why ancient tribes invented such things in the first place."

"They were scaredy-cats!" Nat yelled out.

"Actually, you're right, Nat," Mrs. Wilmont praised him. "But exactly *what* were they afraid of?"

I raised my hand. "Everybody in India used to be

afraid of tigers," I said. "Tigers used to eat more than a thousand people every year there!"

"Are you sure it was that many, Dave?" Mrs. Wilmont asked.

"It's a fact," I said confidently.

"I won't ask for your source, Dave, but you've got the idea. People were afraid and were trying to protect themselves."

"Natives in the jungle were afraid big snakes would drop out of the trees to swallow them whole." Some Nerd called this out, and even before anyone else could react, Nat cheered, "Way to go, man!"

Kids started calling out things to be afraid of, like being struck by lightning, melted in lava flows, and being pulled out to sea by tidal waves. Mrs. Wilmont wrote each one down on the blackboard. "That's some list," she said. "Long ago people made talismans to protect them against all these fears and more!"

"People were scared of finding devils hiding in rocks, or meeting dragons in the woods, or even sailing off the end of the earth because they thought it was flat," Max added.

"Yes, they were," Mrs. Wilmont agreed. "And that's why they needed to believe in charms. Now, why do you think most people no longer use talismans?"

"Because we know a lot about science and other things now," Johnny said.

"Exactly," Mrs. Wilmont said. "The more we know about anything, the less afraid we are of it."

"That's why nothing scares me, because I know everything," Nat brayed. "All these stupid talismans and charms are a big crock!"

Liz raised her hand.

"What is it, Liz?" Mrs. Wilmont asked.

"Do we have to make charms that look like monsters?"

"Certainly not," Mrs. Wilmont said. "Monsters are popular for Halloween, but you can invent anything you want. It can look like anything."

"And if it had nothing to do with monsters, a person could still have a chance to win the lucky Stonehenge coin?" Liz asked.

"Of course," Mrs. Wilmont answered, her face turning more serious. "I'm sure everyone noticed there's no monster on the coin."

"The cranky-looking emperor guy could be a vampire," Johnny suggested.

"He is not," Liz snapped.

"There's a snake," I reminded them.

"There's nothing about the coin that's creepy," Liz insisted.

Mrs. Wilmont opened her desk drawer, and rummaged through it as she spoke. "Do you still have the coin, Liz?" she asked.

"No, Mrs. Wilmont," Liz said, "I put it back."

"Sure," Nat mumbled to Rado.

"Did anyone borrow the Stonehenge coin?" Mrs. Wilmont asked the class, searching as she pulled the drawer out farther.

Nobody said a word.

"I put it back in the left-hand corner where I found it," Liz said.

"It's not here," Mrs. Wilmont announced.

Liz hurried up to the desk. "I put it back *there*," she explained, pointing to the exact spot in the drawer.

Liz and Mrs. Wilmont checked again. I wanted to help so I went up to look under the desk. Before long almost everyone was leaning over looking under their own desks. Kids started getting down on their hands and knees to look under the radiators.

Suddenly, Mrs. Wilmont blew her whistle. "Back to your seats, back to your seats," she ordered. Liz was the last one to sit down. She looked sick to her stomach.

"I'm sorry," Mrs. Wilmont said, her eyes scanning over the entire class, "it seems the Stonehenge coin has disappeared."

Everyone groaned.

"Well, you *said* it was magical." Nat laughed.

I took one look at Nat, and I decided where the coin had probably gone. "Somebody ripped it off," I said, and I looked right at Nat when I said it.

"Right," Nat agreed. "And we all know who wanted that coin more than anyone, don't we?"

"We sure do." Rado snickered.

Before I could blink an eye, practically every kid turned and looked at Liz. Her face turned the color of a cranberry. She looked like she wanted to *die*!

Nat had won this round and there was nothing any of us could do about it.

"I didn't steal the coin," Liz said, choking up. ***"I really didn't."***

I was so furious at Nat and Rado that I didn't know what to do, except try to save Liz.

SIX

Boys and Ghouls, Please Be Sheeted!

I'm sure no one *took* the coin," Mrs. Wilmont assured the class. "I'm certain it'll turn up."

"What if it doesn't because it's been hidden on purpose?" Jennifer said. All the members of the Wacky Facts Lunch Bunch tried to get the heat off Liz by glaring right at Nat.

"It was for the contest." Liz shook her head sadly.

"Coin or no coin, don't worry about monsters," I whispered in Liz's ear. "It's not bad luck because of your fears."

"Now we've got no prize for the best charm," someone whined.

"Nobody can steal a talisman and get away with it," I called out. **"Anybody who rips off a lucky** charm always gets eaten by a ghoul, or some werewolf gets them. They get double bad luck!"

"I'm sure we'll find it," Mrs. Wilmont said. "Now it's time to clean up before the bell."

The kids put the supplies back, walking as if they were at a funeral. The whole thing was a downer. I was glad when the bell rang and the day was over.

I watched as Liz went up to Mrs. Wilmont's desk. I heard her say, "I didn't steal the coin, I really didn't."

"I know you didn't," Mrs. Wilmont reassured her. "It could have fallen into a crack. It could be anywhere. Don't be upset." But Liz was and so was the entire Wacky Facts Lunch Bunch. We decided to do something about it. We walked out together as usual. I saw the Blobs outside in the school yard and we caught up to them.

"You swiped the coin, or you hid it to be mean," I accused Nat flat out.

"I did not," he said, smirking with his big moose face. He pointed at Liz. "I think little *Lizbo's* into five-finger discount now." He always calls her Lizbo when he wants to get her goat.

"You're out of your mind!" Liz shouted.

"You're not going to get away with this frame-up," Johnny told Nat.

"Who says?"

"I'll tell you *who says*!" I interrupted, and said in my most serious voice, **"The coin says!"**

"You're losing your marbles." Nat laughed right in my face.

"No, you lost them once, if you remember," Johnny said, but we didn't go into that.

I quickly added, "When you get a chance to sneak a look, if you just happen to have the coin, you'll see the secret writing on the back of it. We know what it says, because we jotted it down and looked it up." I was fibbing, but I had a very good reason.

"You're nuts!" Nat said. "There's no curse on that coin."

"What does it say?" Rado had fallen for my trap and inspired me to make up a really good curse. I tried to hide my excitement.

"It says if anyone steals the coin, someone's going to *come back* and *get* them!" I said. "That's the curse!"

Rado's eyeballs bulged.

"Someone's going to come back from *where*?" Nat asked.

"From the grave," I said slowly. "That's where. The grave!"

Then I turned and started walking away and the rest of the Wacky Facts Lunch Bunch were in step with me all the way.

"You're a big bull thrower!" Nat yelled after me.

"Some ghost will be back for revenge against the thief who took the coin. Mark my words," I called over my shoulder.

"He means it," Max backed me up. "The coin was really cursed."

"You think I'm an idiot?" Nat shouted. "You wackos all think I'm stupid!"

Jennifer, who loves last licks, added, "**Hey, you two, you've got a couple of really ugly growths on your necks! Oh, excuse me—they're your *heads*!**"

The Nasty Blobs glared like they wanted their looks to kill us. We all stuck together until Nat and Rado vanished into Ronkewitz's candy store across from the school. They always hang out there to play the Killer Commando and Demon Attack video machines in the back.

"I don't like everybody thinking I'm a crook." Liz moaned and moaned and then chewed her hair.

"Everybody knows the Nasty Blobs are responsible, not you," Johnny said.

"No, they don't," Liz insisted.

"I'm really mad," Jennifer said, steaming.

"We don't have time to be mad," I said. "We're going to save Liz's good name and get even! What are friends for, anyway?"

"How can we do that?" Liz perked up.

"My plan is actually simple," I said. "We've got to *really* make sure Houdini's ghost comes back."

"You mean we're going to *fake* it?" Jennifer asked.

"I mean we'll do our best to contact the real ghost of Houdini, but we've got to be ready with a backup, just in case a detail or two doesn't allow Houdini to make it on time," I explained.

"What are you talking about?" Liz asked.

"*Action,* that's what I'm talking about," I said. "*Action!*"

"Yes, Dave, but not *now,*" Jennifer said. "I have to go. My MUTTS BY THE MILE dog-walking service is my responsibility, and I have a neighbor's big collie and a yapping Chihuahua waiting for me. Then I have to help my mom and pop at their store for a change, but I'll call you later." Johnny had to split and Max did, too, but everyone promised to come up with ideas to help Houdini's ghost come back.

"Can I hang out over at your house awhile?" Liz asked.

"Sure," I said. "My mom will even be glad if you want to stay for dinner."

At my house we found a ridiculous sight. Giggles was standing in the living room, wrapping toilet paper around her arms.

"*Hi, Davie,*" she sang. "*Hi, Davie! Hi, Lizzie!*"

"Hi, Giggles," I said.

"What are you doing?" Liz asked her.

"I'm a mummy. A mummy!" Giggles explained, giggling, then she spun on her heels and ran upstairs. She left the carpet covered with pieces of toilet paper.

Liz and I got some food from the kitchen. I zapped us a big bowl of buttered popcorn so Liz wouldn't eat her hair. I could tell she was feeling much better by the time we went to check out my book on Houdini. I wanted her to see all the pictures it had of Houdini doing his tricks.

"He was a great magician?" Liz asked, sitting next to me at my desk, flipping through the book.

"He was more than that. He was the world's greatest escape artist."

"What does that mean?"

"He'd have people put handcuffs on him, and chain him up, and lock him in trunks. Then he'd escape from them in front of audiences," I said. I showed her pictures of him hanging upside down in chains underwater. That was his famous WATER TORTURE ESCAPE stunt.

"Wow!" Liz shoved a whole handful of popcorn into her mouth as she looked at the picture.

"Lots of magicians hated him," I told her.

"Why?"

"Because he exposed their secrets. Houdini always showed audiences how magicians did their tricks." I took the book and plopped on my bunk bed. Liz stretched out on the floor.

"Why did he do that?"

"Because some magicians told people they had real magical powers. They'd say they could contact the dead, and then they charged lots of money. He wanted everyone to know what big fakers they were," I said.

"Let me show you my favorite picture. It's the one of Houdini's family sitting around after he died. They're waiting to hear from him. **He promised he'd contact them from the dead. So far he hasn't.**"

"Then he certainly isn't going to show up at a New Springville Elementary School Fright Party," Liz said, relieved.

"He might."

"How come?"

"Maybe his family all sat around *too late* on Halloween," I suggested. "Maybe lunchtime's a better time. Who knows? But it doesn't matter."

"What do you mean, *it doesn't matter*?" Liz yelled at me. "I confided in you and you don't get it. You know my deepest, most secret fear is that some horrible creature is going to come after me and make me its dinner. If you play with magic, it might show up instead of Houdini's ghost!"

"I'm telling you Houdini's a good ghost."

"I don't want any kind of anything creepy showing up!"

"I'll protect you," I promised. "Think of it this way—you're watching an old Casper the Friendly Ghost cartoon."

Liz shrugged. "I just know that if only I could have Mrs. Wilmont's coin, I'd be better off. That's the only thing that can protect me!"

"You're being silly, especially for someone who's usually so smart and practical."

"I am not."

"Look," I said, "if Houdini hasn't made it back in over forty-five years, you don't have very much to worry about. We've got to be ready with our *own* ghost. We've got to make sure we have a fake ghost so scary Nat Bronski will *plotz*!"

"I can't say I hate your idea. In fact, I'd really like to scare the Blobs. They deserve it." Liz laughed.

I laughed, too. Suddenly, we both couldn't stop laughing. Then I started making eerie ghost sounds. **"BOOOOOOOOOOOOO! BOOOOOOOOOOO!"** Liz got up and started flying around the room, wheezing "BOOOOOOO! BOOOO!" As I loped after her the door to my room opened.

Giggles stood in the doorway with her hands on her hips.

"Davie, I had a worry," she said, staring at me. Her face was all scrunched up. "I don't understand something I heard Mommy tell her friend. *'Don't worry, God is everywhere, even in Peru.'* "

"So what?"

"Well," Giggles said, pouting, **"if God is everywhere, can He see me in the bathroom?** *Can He, Davie? Can He?"*

"I guess I'm not the only one who worries," Liz said, and kept on laughing.

The Abominable Snow Pizza!

Liz got permission to eat dinner at my house. We finished our homework and worked on our ideas for Nightmare Alley.

"My mom's letting me boil a chicken and keep the bones," Jennifer called in. Liz listened in my room, while I was on the extension downstairs.

"We can stick a boiled chicken bone in Nat's hands and tell him it's from a human skeleton!" Jennifer explained.

"Good thinking," I said. *"Nice and nasty."*

"Okay," Liz agreed.

"Liz, you think it's **okay**?" Jennifer asked, puzzled. "I thought you'd think it was revolting."

"It is. But Dave convinced me it's for a good cause," Liz said.

"My father promised to donate a dozen packs

of oozy tofu bean curds from the market," Jennifer added. "You know what tofu feels like when you put your hands in—it feels like gross body fluids!"

"Great," I said.

I wanted to watch *The Fly* on TV at 8:00 P.M. By 7:45 Liz and I had gone through all my Wacky Facts and ghost books and had come up with stuff to get kids in a ghoulish mood. I figured Mrs. Wilmont would let us make copies on her Xerox machine. We could hand them out in the cafeteria. I wrote up TEN WACKY GHOST FACTS, which Liz and I changed so Nat might get really worried:

TEN WACKY GHOST FACTS

compiled by Liz McGinn and Dave Martin

1. A ghost in California made a woman build a house with 347 rooms, 73 bathrooms, and 241 staircases that went nowhere. The ghost told her demons would get her unless she kept a carpenter hammering nails 24 hours a day.

2. A ghost in Sydney, Australia, tortured a nasty kid with toads because he was a liar and a cheat and a thief.

3. Actress Angela Lansbury once stayed in a haunted hotel room and saw the hot water from the faucet turn bloodred.

4. The ghost of a teenager ordered a math teacher to flush eight thousand dollars of her money down the toilet because she gave too many sneak quizzes.

5. The St. James Hotel in Cimarron, New Mexico, still has three terrifying ghosts. You can reserve a room today and go stay there.

6. The ghost of Mary Lewis of Toronto leaves traces of perfume for children she likes. For nasty kids, she leaves boogers.

7. The White House is filled with ghosts. Abraham Lincoln is the most famous one. He walks around his bedroom on the second floor whenever anything really terrible is going to happen to the country.

8. The ghost of Marilyn Monroe appeared on Hollywood Boulevard.

9. The ghost of the famous "Blood Countess" of Hungary appeared at a McDonald's in Budapest and ordered a rare quarter pounder with cheese.

10. Seven ghosts in Hawaii's haunted Waipio Valley cooked a nasty kid who bragged at his school that nothing could scare him.

Liz and I came up with the WACKY FACTS LUNCH BUNCH official invitation to **NIGHTMARE ALLEY.** It was my idea to write it in the *shape of a skull,* but Liz helped a lot with the rest:

ATTENTION!
ATTENTION! ALL KIDS!

The Wacky Facts Lunch Bunch cordially invites
you to meet the **GHOST OF HOUDINI** at Friday's Fright
Party! Houdini, the world's greatest magician and escape artist,
died on Halloween in 1926. He was buried with a telephone. He
promised to come back from the grave. The Houdini Society waits
every Halloween at the Cafe Edison in New York City for Houdini to
return. His family waits at his home for him to call or come back.
Fans wait at his grave in a Queens, New York, cemetery. All believe
he will accomplish his greatest escape feat——an escape from DEATH!
Don't miss the appearance of HOUDINI'S GHOST this Friday in the
lunchroom. He hates liars, and crooks. Especially kids who have
been constantly rotten. Come to a fright-filled visit to our
NIGHTMARE ALLEY lunch table. You will *feel* human
eyeballs, *touch* vampire brains, *taste* a werewolf's body
fluids, *hold* a skeleton's fingers, and discover
other awesome and gruesome Halloween
treats. Come in costume and help us bring
back a real ghost! Be one of the BOO-tiful
people to shudder with terror. Houdini's
ghost will arrive in our lunchroom at the
Friday Fright Party! *It'll be a scream——*
IF YOU'RE NOT TOO SCARED
TO COME!

EIGHT

DEMON-stration!

The next morning the Wacky Facts Lunch Bunch reported for lab squad duty as usual.

"I guess the whole school's into Halloween," Mrs. Wilmont told us. "I don't have a single piece of science equipment on order for delivery today."

"Did anyone turn in the Stonehenge coin?" Liz asked.

"Not yet," Mrs. Wilmont said. "But I'm still hopeful we'll find it."

"Don't worry," I whispered to Liz. "It's a fact that over eighty-three percent of all criminals return to the scene of the crime."

"What does that mean?" Liz asked.

"It means I think if Nat did steal the coin, he won't be happy to sit around and keep it to himself,"

I explained. "Crooks always have to show off what they stole."

"I read in one of my brother's psych books that lots of crooks *want* to get caught," Liz remembered. "You think Nat's like that?"

I nodded. "Definitely. Nat's never happy unless he's caught—you watch!"

"I hope so." Liz looked definitely cheered up.

"Can we use the copy machine for these?" I asked, showing Mrs. Wilmont our notices. She read them and laughed. "Of course. How exciting," she said. "A séance is perfect for a Fright Party."

I looked puzzled. Mrs. Wilmont added, **"A séance is the word used whenever people meet and try to contact the spirit of a dead person."**

"Oh, we're going for more than the spirit," I said, "though a recent Gallup poll showed that sixty-nine percent of Americans and seventy-one percent of the British believe they will go somewhere after death."

"We're going for the whole enchilada," Jennifer explained.

"I know it will be good, clean fun." Mrs. Wilmot walked to her own work desk in the far corner of the lab supply room.

Liz and I showed Max, Johnny, and Jennifer what we'd come up with for handouts. Jennifer handed us each a copy of her favorite monster jokes. "My idea is we pass out what Dave and Liz did this morning. That gets everyone thinking spooky thoughts. Then, at lunch, we pass out my Halloween Ghoulie Foolies."

My three favorite monster jokes on her list were:

1. What does one fifth-grade monster say to another fifth-grade monster that has bubbling slime drooling from its three noses, eight yellow eyes with pus pouring from them, and green skin with leaking, purple, crusty sores?

Answer: **"HI, GOOD-LOOKING!"**

2. What did the vampire ask when he called a funeral home?

Answer: **"DO YOU DELIVER?"**

3. What goes THUMP, THUMP, THUD, CLUMP, SQUISH—THUMP, THUMP, THUD, CLUMP, SQUISH?

Answer: **THE CREATURE FROM THE BLACK LAGOON'S WIFE WITH A WET SNEAKER!**

"Today's Thursday," Liz said, "that means the cafeteria special is frankfurters and sauerkraut. I should have brought something from home."

"Don't you wonder how they always manage to make the sauerkraut look like wiggling maggots?" Johnny asked.

"I don't eat anything that has rodent hairs in it," Jennifer declared.

"Frankfurters *don't* have rodent hairs in them!" Liz said, now defending the gross food.

Jennifer tossed her ponytail. *"Even the companies that make them tell you they have rodent hairs in them!"*

"And pieces of cockroach legs," I added.

Liz gagged. ***"Could we stop this disgusting conversation? Could we?"***

"Johnny, what did you come up with for Nightmare Alley?" Max asked.

"Two things," Johnny said. He dug a piece of paper out of his backpack. "First, I have my usual specialty, *'A REALLY FREAKY THING TO DO!'* "

"What?" I asked eagerly.

"I hope it's better than your last really freaky thing, that PENCIL THROUGH YOUR HEAD." Jennifer sighed.

"Listen up," Johnny said. "This is cool. I call it DEAD CROOK'S HEAD ON A STICK. I wrote down all the directions to make it, so everybody can have a copy."

"It sounds really gross," Liz said.

"It is!" Johnny bragged. "First, you stick a plum on the end of an ice-cream-pop stick," he read from

the paper in his hands. "Then you cut out two eyes, a nose, and a big mouth. You stick the plum in the oven or let it lie around for a few weeks. It gets lots of wrinkles, shrivels up, and gets really dry. Pretty soon it looks like a really gruesome dead crook's face. It's neat."

"It's horrible," Liz said.

"It's great," I said. "Everybody's going to know the dead crook I'm talking about is Nat."

"Oh." Liz thought a minute. "Well, in that case, I guess it *is* a good idea, but no one can do it in school."

"I know that." Johnny read further from his paper, "Enjoy **DEAD CROOK'S HEAD.** Make a dozen of them on pencils and give them as holiday presents. Surprise your friends and the family!"

Max laughed, as he unrolled a computer paper. "I did **CREEPY CARTOONS.**"

We all loved Max's poster. "Let's show it to Mrs. Wilmont," I said. We brought it over to her desk.

"Oh, it's quite wonderful, Max," she said. "May we hang it on our classroom door?"

"Sure," Max said.

The bell rang for us to go to class. We ran to get our books. Suddenly, I remembered Johnny said he had *two* ideas. "What was your other idea?" I asked him.

"*This,*" he said, beckoning us to the high stacks of physics equipment.

"This is my *second* idea," Johnny said mysteriously.

He held an old-fashioned black rotary-dial telephone.

"What?" we all wanted to know.

"I could hook up some batteries and wires to this old phone," he whispered. ***"Then we could make it ring whenever we wanted by just pressing a switch!"***

"Well, then," I said, "I guess that means Houdini will be calling for sure."

"You bet, man." Johnny laughed. ***"You bet!"***

NINE

You Can't Keep a Good Moan Down!

New Springville Elementary School looked like it had gone bananas. Everybody was really getting in the mood for Friday's Fright Party—just one day away! Lots of kids were running around testing out their wax vampire teeth, witch hats, and lots of Dracula, Frankenstein, and werewolf masks even though no one was supposed to. A few kids wore fake noses, and carried rubber snakes and creepy spiders.

In class, Mrs. Wilmont let us pass out copies of our TEN WACKY GHOST FACTS and the NIGHT-MARE ALLEY invitations. Plenty of kids acted really interested. It was great to hear Nat yell out, **"Hey, what's this Houdini garbage?"**

"It's no garbage," I said, making sure his pinhead

brain understood. "We're going to contact his ghost. *We want Houdini to come back from the grave.*"

"I'm really quaking in my boots," Nat said, grinning.

"You ought to be," Johnny told him.

"WEEEEEEEEEEEEEEEEEEE!" Mrs. Wilmont blew her whistle to settle everyone down. The first thing she did was repeat that the Stonehenge coin was still missing.

"So what will I get when I win the *charm* contest?" Nat blurted out.

"What does he get?" Rado repeated like a robot.

"Don't anyone count his or her chickens until they're hatched!" Mrs. Wilmont answered. "I'll pick the winner tomorrow afternoon after the party. If the coin doesn't show up by then, I'll write to my sister in England. She'll buy me another and mail it to our class."

"Your sister lives in England?" a Jock asked.

"She told us that," Jennifer said impatiently.

"Yes," Mrs. Wilmont said. "My older sister lives in the town near Stonehenge where I bought the first coin. I'm certain she'll find another one that will do fine as a prize."

Liz raised her hand. "But it might not be a *magical one.*"

"That's possible," Mrs. Wilmont admitted. "But there is a chance the new coin might even be MORE magical. At least the winner will get a prize."

"I'm definitely going to win!" Nat repeated, clumping a beat-up shopping bag onto his desk. He patted the bag like it was filled with gold. "My charm is gonna blow everybody away! It's a winner!"

"Yeah, Nat's going to win," Rado backed him up.

"I'm pleased to see you are so involved in a project, Nat," Mrs. Wilmont said. "What is it?"

"I want to show mine last," Nat insisted, throwing his arms over the shopping bag. "Let all the dorks go first."

"Always let dorks go first," Rado said.

Mrs. Wilmont gave the Nasty Blobs one of her "cool it" looks.

"I do think we should try to finish up as many talismans this morning as possible. We must decorate the classroom with them," Mrs. Wilmont said. "How many of you have already finished?"

Half the kids in the class raised their hands.

"Wonderful," Mrs. Wilmont said. "We can start with those. The rest of you finish working." She opened the supply cabinet. Liz hurried over to get more clay for what looked like just a lumpy volcano.

"What are you making?" I asked her.

"I don't know," she wailed.

"It looks like it could be some kind of *mountain monster*," I suggested.

"I'm not making any kind of a monster!" she insisted. "And you're the only one who knows

why so don't tell! I'm not going to win *any* coin either! That's the worst part of being afraid of monsters. I'm a big loser!"

"Maybe you'll grow out of being afraid of monsters. Giggles used to be afraid of flies and our neighbor's cat! Just try your best," I encouraged her.

"Baloney," she said. "You sound like my mother."

The first talismans Mrs. Wilmont put on display were Tommy Russo's crepe-paper pizza and Jimmy Quinn's monster silver worm. The pizza had pepperoni eyes and breadstick fangs.

"What kind of charm is it?" Mrs. Wilmont asked Tommy.

"It's a **VAMPIRE PIZZA CHARM,**" he explained. "I want it to put a spell on the cafeteria so they serve pepperoni pizza every day. I love pepperoni pizza."

"Well, I think you've made a very suitable charm, then," Mrs. Wilmont said. She handed out strips of colored paper. "When you're finished making your charm, be sure to write down its name and what kind of powers it has. Tomorrow after the Fright Party we'll have open house. Other classes will come see your wonderful work."

"What's the big stupid, shiny worm?" Nat called out.

"Nat, you were doing so well. Don't ruin your

day by calling anyone's charm *stupid*," Mrs. Wilmont said. "But, what *is* it, Jimmy?"

"It's my **WORM MONSTER CHARM**," Jimmy explained. "I made it to protect me from finding maggots in my candy bars."

"*EEEEEECH!*" The whole class gagged.

"It's healthier than using preservatives," Jennifer spoke up.

I was the first one of the Wacky Facts Lunch Bunch to finish my charm. "It's a skull face. I call it the **HOMEWORK OGRE**," I explained. "It protects me from getting too much homework." Mrs. Wilmont praised it and put it on display. I thought it was in a terrific spot above the aquarium.

Johnny finished his huge **FREDDY KRUEGER CHEESEBURGER.** It was supposed to protect his right to eat junk food. Mrs. Wilmont hung it from the ceiling with a string so it kept twisting and turning spookily.

Jennifer's charm was made from a men's tie box she'd changed into the shape of a dollar sign. "This charm protects my allowance and my earnings from MUTTS BY THE MILE," she said. "It guards all my money—not only from thieves, but I hope from my own greediness!"

I really liked it and I knew it was right-on because Jennifer is the official Treasurer of the Wacky Facts Lunch Bunch.

"What an imaginative idea," Mrs. Wilmont told her.

"Thanks," Jennifer said. "I hope it also brings me more customers for MUTTS BY THE MILE," she added. "I can't make a living with just a collie and a Chihuahua."

By the period before lunch almost all the kids had finished their charms and turned them in. Mrs. Wilmont displayed them all around the classroom. Some of the Jocks came up with baseballs and footballs that looked like vicious kinds of fish. One Brain made a **REPORT CARD MONSTER** that had claws and a long, hairy tongue.

Max's **FRIENDSHIP CHARM** made perfect sense to me. He was still glad to have the Wacky Facts Lunch Bunch for friends. Even though his mother had died and he had a vampire father, he had us. His charm ended up being a big Valentine face but he used his cartoon style and made it have a shrieking gorilla's mouth. I figured it had a good chance to win the contest. It was better than my skull and the pizza monster. I thought it was better than everybody's because Max knows how to draw so well.

Finally, we were waiting for only three kids to finish.

One was Liz.

By midmorning her charm still looked lame.

"I need more time," Liz begged Mrs. Wilmont.

"That's fine, Liz," Mrs. Wilmont said, calming her. "You can still work after lunch."

"Thank you," Liz said.

"It looks like some kind of *jar*," Jennifer said.

"Maybe it's a vase," Max offered.

Mrs. Wilmont walked toward the back of the room. She stopped at Rado's desk. "Will you need more time, too?" she asked the mouse.

"Nope," Rado squeaked. He reached into his shirt pocket and took out a tiny *clay figure*. It looked like something a two-year-old kid would make in ten seconds. He beamed as he put it in Mrs. Wilmont's hand.

"It's so small," Mrs. Wilmont said.

*"You didn't say our charms had to be **big**!"* Nat butted in, sticking up for his buddy boy.

"You're right, what is it?" Mrs. Wilmont asked Rado.

"A voodoo dwarf," Rado gurgled.

"Is that like a voodoo *doll*?" Mrs. Wilmont asked.

Rado scrunched up his face like he'd just gotten a sniff of bad cheese. "It's no *doll*."

"What does it protect you from?" Mrs. Wilmont wanted to know.

"From what's in Nat's *shopping bag*," Rado said, letting out a shrill laugh.

Mrs. Wilmont turned to Nat. She looked really curious now. "What *is* in your bag?" she asked him. "Are you ready to show us?"

"This." Nat grinned. He carefully lifted up a painted clay face the size of a dinner plate.

The whole class gasped.

Even Mrs. Wilmont looked shocked.

Nat had made a red face with horns, nasty eyes, and a mouth filled with yellow, broken teeth. It was an incredibly scary face.

"Oh, my," Mrs. Wilmont said. "Is that supposed to be what I think it is?"

"Yep," Nat said in a little kid's voice. "It's a bad, *bad* boy!"

Nat had made a really excellent devil face. It looked alive and ready to attack.

"He's a cutie, isn't he?" Nat laughed, tickling the devil's chin.

"Nat wins, right?" Rado giggled in Mrs. Wilmont's face.

"W-w-well . . ." she stammered.

"You're surprised, aren't you?" Nat laughed. "You thought I'd make something crummy."

Mrs. Wilmont took a deep breath. "Nat, you're very talented when you want to be. I've told you that before," she admitted. "You obviously make good *devils*. Now, what does it *do* so that you selected it as your talisman?"

"It watches out for me." Nat smiled, petting the devil's brow. *"It protects me."*

"From what?" Mrs. Wilmont asked.

"From being a scaredy-cat like the rest of the wimps in this class." Nat laughed. "So I win, right?"

"Well . . ." Mrs. Wilmont was looking around the classroom, obviously trying to figure out what to reply.

"Hey, Mrs. Wilmont," I called out, *"Liz hasn't finished her charm yet! She still has a chance, you know!"*

"You're right, Dave," Mrs. Wilmont said quickly. "We'll have to wait until all the projects are done before I pick the winner. And, as I told you, I'll announce the winner *after* tomorrow's party."

Everybody turned quickly to see how Liz's charm was coming along. We all seemed surprised the lump of clay in front of her was starting to look like something.

"What is it?" Nat brayed.

"I don't know," Liz confessed. "I just don't know."

"I can wait." Nat laughed like crazy, clutching his devil face. *"But I'm going to be the winner, folks! I'm going to be the winner!"*

►T E N◄

Raising Spirits!

"That is _so_ revolting," Jennifer complained as we all went down the stairs for lunch. "Nat _stole_ one Stonehenge coin, and now he's going to WIN another one."

Liz was obviously so upset she was not paying attention. Not only was she fiddling with her necklace, which suddenly broke, she missed a step and all the shiny blue diamonds and mirrored beads spilled from her neck and bounced down the stairs. Some of us ran around picking up the pieces, and Johnny helped her up.

"I'm such a loser," she moaned. "Such a loser."

"No, you're not," I insisted.

"You're the only one who's got a chance to beat Nat," Johnny pointed out.

"How am I going to beat Nat with a dumb lump of clay?" Liz asked.

"It was starting to look like an *interesting* lump of clay," Max said.

Liz grumbled, *"I don't even know what it is!"*

"It could be a great work of modern art," I said. "Most sculptures by great artists today are totally weird and nobody knows what they are!"

Max, Liz, and I got in the cafeteria line to buy our lunch. We ended up with the special, which looked like a hairy omelet. I was interested in taking another close look at the steam table. I needed to check out the four little red heat lights above the table. I figured they'd make a nice touch when all the shades were drawn.

Most important of all, I needed to find out if the steam table would be too hot for one of us to hide under it for the Fright Party. The one thing I knew for sure was that I was going to make Houdini's ghost come back to get Nat, one way or another.

Mrs. Rowan noticed me close to the steam table. "Can I get you anything?" She smiled her grandmotherly smile.

"I was just wondering how hot the steam table is," I said. "You know, we might need it on Friday for the Fright Party."

"Oh, it won't be hot tomorrow," Mrs. Rowan said. "We're having a cold buffet."

"How come?" Max asked.

"We're serving only special Halloween treats," Mrs. Rowan said.

"Like what?" Liz wanted to know.

"Well," Mrs. Rowan said, "let me see. We're making cat-and-bat-shaped baloney sandwiches, macaroni salad, witch cookies, goblin Jell-O, pumpkin pie, a haunted-house cake, and a few surprises."

"Great," we all said as I checked *under* the steam table.

"Could someone fit underneath?" Max asked.

Mrs. Rowan laughed and scratched her head. "Sure," she said. "Someone small."

"Do you think we could use the red lights, too," I asked.

"Anything for Halloween," she said, showing me the switch on the side.

All I could think of was what a swell altar the steam table was going to be.

We brought our trays to our table. I called the Wacky Facts Lunch Bunch to order. We got right to a checklist for Nightmare Alley and the appearance of Houdini's ghost.

"I'm bringing in the eyeballs, chicken bones, and the tofu body fluids," Jennifer said. "I can also bring in a squashy tomato, which will feel like a pygmy's brain."

"Great," Johnny said. "I'll bring in the slimy spaghetti. I tested it out and it's better if I cut it into little pieces. Before kids stick their hands in the bowl, we can tell them it's worms that ate their way out of a dead man's body."

Liz covered her mouth with her hand. "You are all going to make me throw up!"

"Hey, we've got to be organized," I reminded her.

Johnny continued, "I'll also be in charge of batteries and wires so we can make the Houdini telephone ring whenever we want."

"That's going to be great," Max said. "My father bought a new rug for our living room. We saved one of the small scraps. I'll bet that if we put grease on that, in the dark it will feel like a dead ghoul's scalp."

"All of this is so gross," Liz said, shivering, and the shiny stones and beads she was trying to restring onto her broken necklace kept dropping.

"Liz, do you want to get even with Nat, or not?" I asked.

Liz's forehead wrinkled, and after a moment she said defiantly, *"I want to get even!"*

"What we definitely need are some phony vapors for the arrival of our ghost," I said. "I happen to know it's a fact that if we put dry ice in water, it makes great vapors."

"I can get some dry ice," Johnny said. "The ice-cream store near me should have plenty."

"What if Houdini's *real* ghost shows up?" Liz asked, and she looked really worried. I knew how afraid Liz was, and I respected the fact that she just wasn't ready to tell the others about her worst fear —but there was no way I wanted to stop the Fright Party or stop all our great plans.

"If the real ghost shows up we can skip the dry ice." Max laughed. "Also, I can bring rope to hang the sheets and blankets up for Nightmare Alley. My dad said he could get us old U.S. Navy sheets and blankets from the Navy base."

"I can take care of THE MUMMY'S HAND and flashlights," I said. It seemed so well organized and exciting I felt like cheering.

"But what kind of costumes are we going to wear?" Liz asked.

"We forgot about that." Jennifer looked doubtful. "I don't want to spend a lot of money. I'm working too hard to make it."

Johnny agreed.

Suddenly, an idea hit me. Liz caught the look in my eye. "Dave, what's going on in your head?"

"We can *all* go as **the ancient people of Stonehenge—the Druids! Druids wore ROBES!**" I cried out.

"Is this a Wacky Fact, Dave?" Liz asked. "Because this isn't the time."

"What kind of robes?" Jennifer asked.

"Sheets," I said. "They were all little guys who used to run around Stonehenge doing sacrifices and all the things that needed to be done."

"I can get plenty of sheets," Max reminded us.

Liz complained, "We'll just look like dopey fake ghosts if we just wear sheets."

"We could tie-dye them," Jennifer said.

"Yes," Johnny said. "Black. We could dye them black. **Black will make us look scary.**"

"Black, but with white spiderweb tie-dye designs," Jennifer added excitedly. "I learned how to tie-dye at camp last summer! No sweat!"

After lunch Mrs. Wilmont led the class outside for our gym period. Everyone except Liz. Mrs. Wilmont let her stay to finish her charm.

"When the bell rang to go back to class, everyone was exhausted. Mrs. Wilmont was the first one to notice Liz had finished her charm.

"Oh, my," Mrs. Wilmont said as she approached Liz's desk. "What an interesting-looking talisman," she said.

Jennifer, Max, Johnny, and I looked and we were really surprised. Soon, the whole class was staring.

The clay creation Liz had shaped was a big bowl, but Liz had molded wings onto it. Wings and an *angel's head* with long hair rose up from one side of it. A bunch of little hands were all around the rim. They looked like cherub hands. The best part, though, was the whole bowl looked like it was on *fire.* The afternoon sun blazed in through the windows, hitting the blue diamonds and mirrored beads Liz had pressed *into* the clay.

"It's very magical, Liz," Mrs. Wilmont said. "Very magical."

The way all the kids were whispering I could tell practically everyone thought it was a lot better than Nat's mean, ugly thing.

"What is it, Liz?" Mrs. Wilmont asked.

"I still don't know." Liz sighed.

"Ha! Ha!" Nat yelled. "Then she can't win! You've got to know what it is to win!"

"Right, Mrs. Wilmont? Right?" Rado squeaked.

"Liz's is the best charm!" I blurted out. **"It doesn't matter if she doesn't know what it is! It's great!"**

"Right!" Johnny agreed.

"Right!" Max and Jennifer chimed in together.

"Dream on, you losers," Nat said, sneering. *"Dream on!"*

Suddenly, Liz turned to face Nat. She didn't look angry. She looked grateful.

"Thank you, Nat," she said excitedly.

"For what?" Nat wanted to know.

"For letting me know what my charm is!" she exclaimed.

Nat's moose mouth dropped open.

Liz looked to Mrs. Wilmont. **"I *do* know what it is now,"** Liz cried out.

"What?" Mrs. Wilmont asked.

"It's a *Dream Catcher*!" Liz said. *"It's a Dream Catcher to hold and protect all my dreams!"*

ELEVEN

Super Natural!

The next morning I was freaked out of my gourd. I hadn't slept much because I had nightmares. Nat's devil kept chasing Liz's Dream Catcher and trying to eat it. By the time I came down to breakfast, I knew I'd be really bananas if Nat's charm won the contest.

"Davie, Davie." Giggles followed me around while I tried to make an English muffin and chugalug a glass of orange juice. Dad and Mom were getting ready to go to work.

"Davie, if I can get a pass, can I come to your party?" Giggles asked sweetly. *"Can I, Davie, can I?"*

"No," I said, firmly. "The first and second graders have their own party in the auditorium. The one in the lunchroom is going to be too scary for little kids! And I've told you a million times, call me Dave, not *Davie!*"

"I'm going to be a toilet-paper mummy!" she repeated. *"I'm going to be a toilet-paper mummy!"*

"Mom," I yelled to my mother who was no longer in the kitchen, **"I'm taking the yellow rubber dishwashing gloves. I need them for the Fright Party."**

"I need them, too, Davie," Giggles told me, and she was giggling.

"No you don't. What for?"

"Yes, Davie. They are for me."

"Look, Giggles, I'll take you TRICK OR TREATING after school. You can use them then."

I grabbed the yellow gloves from under the sink and threw them in the shopping bag with my other supplies. I put on my costume. The sheets had all come out dark except for spooky white spiderwebs down the front. They didn't look like sheets at all but were great spooky robes.

I ran upstairs to get my backpack. I kissed my mom, dad, and Darwin good-bye.

"Enjoy the party, Dave," Mom said, throwing me another kiss.

"Knock 'em dead with THE MUMMY'S HAND," Dad urged, "and remember to use a lot of cold cream and grease."

"Thanks, Dad."

Darwin gave me a last lick, and rolled over for a nap.

I headed to school.

Liz was waiting for me at the corner of Richmond Avenue and Elm Street, and I thought she looked terrific in her robe. She was wearing so many necklaces and bracelets she jangled as she walked.

"What's with all the jewelry?" I asked.

"Do you still expect me to tell fortunes?"

"Sure."

"Well, then, I'm also a fortune-telling *gypsy*," she said. "The jewelry will go with the turban I'll make out of my mother's scarf."

"Way to go," I said. "Did you work on a really nasty fortune to tell Nat?" I helped her carry her backpack while she lugged *two* shopping bags.

"I'm not going to tell anyone anything too scary."

"But you're an actress, right?" I said. "Just make believe you're some kind of a witch who can see the future."

"I don't play witches and I hate scary parts."

"But you could."

"You're lucky I'm doing this at all. I still think that drooling ape-lizard monster with the needle teeth is going to show up and digest me to death," Liz whispered.

"Don't be silly."

"I checked another of my brother's psych books last night. There are cases about people who saw monsters. Lots of people have seen the one in Loch Ness, and now another one's turned up in Vermont! The book said people have seen monsters all over the place!" she insisted.

"No big deal. Just live and let live, right?"

"If I only had the magic coin, I just know it'd protect me. Maybe Nat didn't steal it. Maybe Mrs. Wilmont found it!" Liz said.

"Even if the coin did show up, Mrs. Wilmont said she wasn't going to award it until after the Fright Party," I reminded her.

"I still hope my Dream Catcher wins!"

Lots of the kids were wearing their costumes to school. In front was a girl I recognized from Giggles's second-grade class who was dressed as a wedding cake. She had bride-and-groom dolls on top of her head. Other kids were dressed as trolls, penguins, Batwoman, bunnies, jack-o'-lanterns, pirates, and cowboys.

The Wacky Facts Lunch Bunch *Druids* gathered just inside the front entrance. We marched as a group up to the laboratory supply room.

"Good morning," Mrs. Wilmont greeted us.

Mrs. Wilmont was dressed as an Arabian princess with harem pants and a beaded headband.

"Oh, you look beautiful," Jennifer told her.

"I love your skeleton earrings," Liz said.

"Why, thank you," Mrs. Wilmont replied, beaming. "And who are you all?"

"Druids," Max told her.

"How perfect for Halloween!" She laughed.

None of the teachers needed any science supplies, so we had lots of time to put our plan into action. Jennifer and Liz took all the bowls, pans, and dry ice that had to be refrigerated down to the cafeteria. Mrs. Rowan had said it was okay.

Johnny set up the batteries and wires for the old telephone. Max and I needed to prepare the ropes and blankets for Nightmare Alley. We wanted everything ready so it could go up fast.

We had to put the telephone on the steam table, and cover it with a white sheet. We needed to put a pail of water under the table for the vapors to appear when it came time to make the dry-ice spooky fog. Everything had to be ready for Houdini's ghost and the best Fright Party anyone had ever heard about in fifth grade!

Everyone *OOOOOHED* and *AAAAHED* when we walked into our classroom and they saw Mrs. Wilmont as an Arabian princess with the Halloween touch of skeleton earrings! There were a lot of great costumes and gimmicks, too. Somebody wore twenty battery-operated Halloween lights on his head and the lights kept flashing.

There were five vampires, three wolfmen, two

pom-pom girls, three ninjas, two ballerinas, a skunk, and a gorilla. Lots of the other kids had masks, Dracula blood kits, scary tattoos, tinsel rock-star wigs, a "Chucky" makeup kit, goggle glasses, and painted faces. The best part was that everyone was acting nuts and no one told us to keep it down or cut it out. **It was going to be a party Houdini or any dead celebrity would *really* want to come back to!**

"Attention! Attention!" Mrs. Wilmont finally clapped her hands.

When that didn't work, she blew her famous and noisy whistle: **"WEEEEEEEEEEEEEEEEE-EEE!"**

Everyone shut up pretty quickly.

"Remember the party doesn't start until lunch period. We still have a lot of schoolwork to do this morning," she announced.

Everybody groaned.

Mrs. Wilmont's favorite subject is science, and she teaches that every day. I was so spaced-out I could hardly concentrate.

"WHAT IS AN ECLIPSE?" is what I finally noticed she'd written on the blackboard. Then Mrs. Wilmont brought out two pumpkins and a flashlight.

"Let's say the big pumpkin is the earth," she said, "and the little one is the moon." She pulled the shades down. "And we'll pretend this flashlight is the sun." She turned the light on and moved the beam toward the pumpkins.

"Does anyone know what a *lunar* eclipse is?" Mrs. Wilmont asked.

"I do," Johnny said. "It's when the shadow of the earth moves across the moon so you can't see the moon for a while."

"Can you show us, Johnny?" she asked.

"Sure." He took the flashlight and moved it so it was on one side of the *earth pumpkin,* which cut off the light reflecting from the *moon pumpkin.*

"Excellent," Mrs. Wilmont said as Johnny handed her back the flashlight. "And what do we call the kind of eclipse that used to *really* frighten ancient peoples?"

Over a dozen kids raised their hands and called out at the same time, "A *solar* eclipse."

"Right again," Mrs. Wilmont said. She moved the beam of light slowly behind the moon so it cast a shadow on the earth. "People, just like the ones who lived near Stonehenge, would sometimes find themselves in this shadow zone. In the middle of the day it would suddenly become night. How do you think that made them feel?"

"Scared," Liz said.

"Yes," Mrs. Wilmont agreed. "Terrified. Just imagine how frightening it must have been for people to see the sun blotted out and find themselves plunged into darkness—without knowing why."

"People have always been scared of shadows," I called out excitedly. "At funerals in China, mourners used to stand back so their shadows wouldn't get caught in a coffin. And lots of dogs don't like a kite shadow to pass over their heads because they think it's a hawk coming down to grab them!"

"You're right, Dave," Mrs. Wilmont said. "But who knows what lots of smart people do today when they're afraid of something?"

"They close their eyes." Nat laughed.

"No, they don't," Mrs. Wilmont corrected.

Max raised his hand. "Smart people tell other people about their fears," he said.

"Exactly." Mrs. Wilmont nodded. "They talk about them and compare them. And then they do something about them. When I was at Stonehenge I saw the magnificent, huge stones an ancient people erected so they could understand day and night, winter and spring—and be able to predict eclipses. They placed the stones in a great circle so the sun would cast shadows on them and tell them things they needed to know so they didn't have to be so frightened."

Liz looked like she wanted to ask something, but didn't. I raised my hand. "What about people who are afraid of monsters and nightmares? What should they do?"

"Well, that brings us right back to Halloween, doesn't it?" Mrs. Wilmont smiled. "We should always express our fears. We can make objects, like our talismans, to help us understand our feelings. And we can speak our fears. That's the best way to get rid of them."

"What if someone told someone their worst fear, but it still didn't go away?" I asked. I looked at Liz out of the corner of my eye. She was all ears waiting for Mrs. Wilmont's answer.

Suddenly, Mrs. Wilmont put the flashlight under her chin. Stark shadows streamed up her face, making her look like a hideous ghoul. Lots of kids gasped at how scary it made her look.

Mrs. Wilmont laughed. "If there's one thing I've learned about life," she said, "it's that the more people I share my fears with, the more they disappear." She moved the flashlight slowly up and away from her face until we could see her beautiful smile again. "Just telling others about your secret nightmares lets the light shine in."

I could really see why everyone says Mrs. Wilmont is the best teacher in the school!

The lunch bell rang.

The sounds on the staircase were like a herd of elephants stampeding. Obviously, everyone couldn't wait to start scaring each other. Lots of the kids were already biting capsules so they could drool fake blood. It seemed that hundreds of plastic fangs were grinning from mouths.

Once we hit the lunchroom, Johnny, Max, and I

ran at top speed to our table. We got the ropes and blankets up right away just like a circus tent. Jennifer and Liz got all our surprises out of the refrigerator. As Mrs. Wilmont and the rest of the teachers sat off to one side sipping coffee and sampling bat-shaped sandwiches, the place was a madhouse.

While everybody fed their faces, Miss Vroom announced she would play the piano. Suddenly, we heard "Dem Bones, Dem Bones, Dem Dry Bones!" Her second selection was "Swan Lake." "Why would she play the music from a ballet at a Fright Party?" Jennifer asked. I told everyone the Wacky Fact that it was the theme music played in *The Mummy* movie.

All of us in the Wacky Facts Lunch Bunch gobbled some lunch and candy while we continued to set up.

Kids at several other tables had decided to put on fright shows, too. Joan and her group from Ms. Gale's class ran a spooky quiz show called *ABC'S from the Crypt!* They gave a candy bar for every correct answer to monster movie trivia questions. The Jocks ran a **SLAM DUNK FOR APPLES** event at their table. Believe it or not, some kids loved leaning over the tub of floating apples while the Jocks shoved their heads under cold water.

"Did you know the Wacky Fact that it was the ancient Druids who had invented dunking for apples?" I asked the Jocks.

"No," the Jock ringleader Perry Tailette answered.

"Well, they did," I assured him. "It was believed that if you caught a floating apple with your teeth it meant the next year would bring a good harvest."

I noticed that even Nat and Rado looked like they were having a ball. They were mainly tripping Nerds and passing out pepper chewing gum. When they weren't doing that, they were pressing windup buzzers on kids' heads.

Finally, when all the cafeteria shades were pulled shut, the lunchroom was as spooky as a haunted house. There was just enough light to see what was going on. Thanks to the blankets, the inside of our **NIGHTMARE ALLEY** was pitch black. We were ready.

Johnny, Liz, Jennifer, Max, and I held flashlights under our chins.

Suddenly, Liz, who had seemed much calmer since Mrs. Wilmont's eclipse discussion, whispered to me, **"I have this awful feeling my horrid nightmare monster is still going to show up! I'm scared!"**

"Don't be," I whispered back. "Remember what Mrs. Wilmont explained. Maybe you should tell the rest of the kids in our club."

"No," she barked.

"Don't worry," I tried to reassure her. "We've planned everything. Don't panic."

As we lined up in our tie-dyed spiderweb robes I know we looked spooky. Everybody hushed and all eyes turned to us.

"NIGHTMARE ALLEY IS NOW OPEN FOR VISITORS!" I bellowed in my best creepy voice. Then Johnny added in a real spooky voice, *"NO KIDS WITH HEART CONDITIONS WILL BE ADMITTED!"*

"What a crock!" Nat yelled out, trying to break the mood.

Plenty of kids rushed to line up at our NIGHTMARE ALLEY tent. Even Mrs. Wilmont and Ms. Gale lined up. Everyone wanted a good scare. We hurried to man our battle stations.

I was scared—not because it was spooky, but because I wanted everything to work perfectly.

Hanna Bell from Mr. Cohen's class was our first victim. Liz, now in her gypsy outfit, made Hanna pick a tarot card out of a deck.

"Hanna," Liz said, looking at the card and sounding really nervous, "something very creepy is going to happen to you."

Hanna looked at Liz's hands and saw they were actually *shaking*. She must have picked up on the vibes that Liz was genuinely spooked. Hanna *screamed*! We hadn't even pulled any of the heavy-duty stuff and Hanna Bell was already screaming. In fact, she screamed the whole time she was in Nightmare Alley. We were off to a great start!

Carlos Garcia was next in line. He picked a tarot card.

"This card tells me you'd better not soap any windows or throw rotten eggs tonight on the street, because you'll get caught," Liz said, her hand still shaking.

"Ha Ha! Big deal!" Carlos said, and moved on to Jennifer. She gave him a wicked smile. **"Carlos, give me your hand. You are now going to feel a bowlful of eyeballs,"** Jennifer said, imitating a witch's cackle. *"Vaya con Dios!"*

She guided Carlos's hand into the slimy bowl. When Carlos screamed really loud, some of the other kids waiting in line screamed *before* they even got into NIGHTMARE ALLEY.

Next, Timmy Warner got all the way past Liz's fortune and Jennifer's eyeballs without a peep. But then he reached Max. Max warned him that he was going to feel human skeleton fingers. Then Max opened Jimmy's hands and plopped the two chicken bones in them. In the pitch black Timmy shrieked!

The kids who didn't scream when they were told about the bones definitely screamed when they reached the **pygmy's brain,** a soft, squashy tomato in a rough-bottom bowl. And if that didn't get a re-action, the oozing dead man's scalp and spaghetti worms did. Liz's fortunes weren't very spooky, but kids were leaving our Alley scared to death.

Then Nat and Rado finally got in line.

"Hey, you screaming meemies!" Nat called out to everyone else, *"this is all a big crock. Nothing scares me!"*

Since Nat had called for everyone's attention, there was a hushed lunchroom when the Nasty Blobs entered NIGHTMARE ALLEY. Everyone wanted to hear if the bragging bullies Nat and Rado would scream like chickens.

I rushed to Liz's side and whispered in her ear, **"Come on. You can do it. To get even, we need everything going for us. Tell them really gross fortunes! We're counting on you!"**

"I don't think I can. Each person has only made me feel more anxious. I hate monsters, and I don't like this one bit," Liz said. *"I just can't!"*

Rado was first. He picked a tarot card and gave it to Liz. She looked at it, and then at Rado. I could see she was thinking about the monster from her nightmares and wondering if it was going to appear instead of Houdini.

"This is the card of bad luck," Liz started, her voice quivering.

"Is that all?" Rado laughed.

"You will have very b-b-bad luck," Liz stuttered.

"Don't believe her," Nat told him. "That's a load of bull." He'd pushed in with Rado.

"I don't believe her," Rado squeaked, and then moved on to Jennifer's area of Nightmare Alley.

"I have a special treat for you, Rado," Jennifer told him, in a creepy voice.

"What?" Rado asked in almost a whisper.

"On the way here today a container fell out of an undertaker's van," Jennifer said. "I want you to feel what was in that container. Something strange. Something frightening. Something just for you." Jennifer waited for just the right moment, and then rammed Rado's hand into the slimy grapes and shrieked, "They're eyeballs! Eyeballs!"

"EHHHHHHHHHHHHHH!" Rado screamed. He didn't even finish the rest of Nightmare Alley. He just ran back to his table, trembling like the mouse he is.

Now there was only Nat. *"Come on, let's get this phony baloney over with!"* he ordered.

Liz looked and sounded more frightened than ever. "Pick a tarot card," she said, her voice breaking.

"Don't waste your hocus-pocus on me," Nat sneered, but he picked a card out of the deck and handed it to Liz. That was when he made a very big mistake. I saw him flash a yellowish and rusty coin at her as if to confuse her.

Nat gave Liz a big, nasty grin, and the coin disappeared again. *"You and I can scare each other!"* he said, snickering.

The fear on Liz's face faded. Her eyes opened

wide. "Wait, you've got the magic coin," I heard her tell him angrily.

"Naw, you were seeing things." Nat laughed.

"I just saw it, I know I did!" Liz insisted. Now she looked furious. For a second I thought she was going to smack him or grab him and search him. Instead, a strange, wide smile slowly crept across her face. ***"So this is your card, Nat?"***

I didn't know what she was up to, but her voice had completely stopped shaking.

"Yeah," Nat answered.

"What I see in your card is *frightening*," she told him.

Nat laughed again. "Well, I don't feel too frightened, so what is it?"

"I'm afraid to tell you. In fact, I don't think I should tell you," Liz said. I could tell she was switching into her full actress **I'VE-GOT-THE-AUDIENCE'S-ATTENTION-AND-I-LOVE-IT** behavior.

"Aw, go on," Nat said, still chuckling.

"You asked for it, so here goes—something **terrible** is going to happen to you, Nat," she told him.

"What?"

Liz took a deep breath. She stared at the card like she really knew what she was talking about. "The card you've picked is the Dark Prince card."

"What?"

"It's a very unfortunate card," Liz said slowly. "This card only appears when a long-gone person is going to return from the grave."

"Like Houdini?" Nat laughed. "You guys are so dumb."

"Maybe. Maybe worse," Liz said. "The spirit world is angry because you've been evil. You've done things to hurt a lot of other kids. Something horrible is after you, waiting for you." Liz began to shake again, but this time I knew she was acting. She lowered her voice. "You've been guilty, Nat, and some terrible thing is going to leave its grave and come for you."

Liz raised her voice so lots of kids could hear. I began to realize she was taking Mrs. Wilmont's advice to tell others about her worst fear. Lots of others! Only she just decided to make it *Nat's*! **It has fur, and claws—and the most horrible thing is its head. Half of it is a face that's no longer human, and the other half is a grizzled lizard's. Its mouth is hideous, with huge, yellow needle teeth and awful juices dripping from it. It's a monstrous beast!" Liz suddenly stood up and screamed. "It's horrible! Something really horrible is coming for you, Nat! I CAN'T GO ON! IT'S TOO TERRIBLE!"**

Everyone turned to see what Nat would do. He stood up. He tried to smile, but Liz had really shaken him. I could tell from the pleased expression on her face she'd faced her fears about her own nightmare, and had done a very good job of giving it to Nat!

"That fortune is dumb! This whole thing—you and your club—it's really dumb." Nat started to swagger through the rest of NIGHTMARE ALLEY, but it seemed to me his mouth was quivering and he looked worried. He went through, touched the eyeballs, bones, and even the dead man's scalp, but they didn't make him scream.

I signaled the Wacky Facts Lunch Bunch into a huddle.

"Great, Liz!" I whispered.

"Terrific," Jennifer, Johnny, and Max agreed.

"Thanks." Liz beamed.

"But now it's time for Houdini!" I gave the sign and we all knew what that meant.

TWELVE

Ouch! Eeeeeek! Ugh!

There were less than fifteen minutes left for the Fright Party. The cafeteria food service had closed down and the staff had cleaned up so the kitchen was dark.

Johnny grabbed me. "Where's the rubber glove for the MUMMY'S HAND!"

"In my shopping bag," I whispered.

"Where?" Johnny asked, really worried.

I pointed my flashlight to where I'd last seen my bag, but I couldn't find it.

"What're we going to do?" Johnny asked.

"You've got to do something else!" I urged. "Just make sure you scare a scream out of Nat!"

Jennifer, Liz, Max, and I came out from Nightmare Alley and pretended we wanted everyone to feel the eyeballs and maggots again. It caused just enough shrieks and fuss so that Johnny was able to slip out the side exit.

We had timed it so he'd need no more than two minutes to run up to the first floor, across the auditorium, and then down the back staircase closest to the kitchen. Then he was supposed to hide under the steam table. I figured maybe he'd grease up his own hand and it'd be enough to scare Nat when the time came.

At last I spotted Johnny as he crept through the kitchen shadows to the steam table.

"YOUR ATTENTION, EVERYONE! ATTENTION, PLEASE!" I called out like the ringmaster of a three-ring spook circus. **"As we promised, the time has come for us to attempt to contact Houdini's ghost!"**

"Another crock," Nat said, but he still sounded rattled from Liz's fortune. Rado wasn't so sure it was a crock, so he hung back. Mrs. Wilmont caught my eye and gave me a big wink.

I walked up to the steam table, allowing my robe to whirl. I switched on the top four red lights of the steam table like Mrs. Rowan had shown me. Everyone's gaze was fixed on me as I pulled the cover sheet off the steam table. There in plain sight was the old black telephone.

"As you know," I reminded everyone, "Houdini— the greatest magician and escape artist in the world —was buried with a telephone. I need your help!

First, we need total silence. I want us all to concentrate very hard now and ask Houdini to contact us."

"Sure." Nat burped loud, then laughed like the moose he is and said, "I'll bet Houdini's *dying* to talk to us!"

"Be quiet," someone called.

Liz, Jennifer, and Max came up carrying a chair. Max set the chair down.

"Since nothing scares Nat," I announced, "I'm sure he won't be too chicken to sit up close to greet the ghost."

Nat looked at me, then at the crowd of kids waiting to see what he was going to do.

"Piece of cake," he brayed, walking to the chair and sitting down smack in front of the steam table.

A couple of CLINK and CLANK sounds came from the table. I knew it was Johnny dropping the dry ice into the pail of water. Within seconds, everyone could hear bubbling and see white, thick vapors spilling out from under the table.

"Big deal." Nat laughed when he saw the vapors. "Dry ice!"

"Silence!" I called out. I moved my robed arms up and down a few times, pretending to be doing magic. Liz moved to my side.

"O ghost of Houdini, please contact us!" she cried out. Her acting was so good she started to scare me.

Next, Max, Jennifer, Liz, and I, right foot first,

began to move slowly in a circle. **"We believe you can escape from the grave, Houdini! We believe in it!"** we started chanting.

Everybody kept one eye on the phone.

"Call us, Houdini!" I said.

"Yes, phone us from your coffin!" Jennifer said.

"Now, O ghost! Now!" Liz cried out. The room was so quiet you could hear a pin drop when, **suddenly, the phone rang.**

Lots of kids screamed.

Out of the corner of my eye I saw Nat looked worried.

He stood up and walked to the telephone. He lifted the whole thing up, saw the wires and followed them to the battery on the floor.

"Who are you jokers kidding!" Nat said, yanking the wires off the battery. *"Who connected the batteries? Who's sticking dry ice in water? Who's hiding in there?"*

Nat yanked open the doors under the steam table.

Johnny looked really embarrassed as he climbed out.

"Talk about lame," Nat blurted.

He laughed so hard he had to sit down on the chair again. He just laughed and laughed, with Rado squeaking along with him. We, the Wacky Facts Lunch Bunch, just stood there feeling foolish. We figured we had really lost.

Suddenly, there was a loud crash from the blackness of the kitchen.

Everyone jumped, even Nat.

Someone, or **something,** had knocked over a big stack of pans. Something was crawling from the darkness toward the red, eerie light of the steam table. Everyone knew the Wacky Facts Lunch Bunch had nothing to do with it, because the five of us were in plain sight. Mrs. Wilmont and the other teachers moved closer. **The something moved along the floor. It came closer and closer, heading straight for Nat.**

"It's something from a grave!" Jennifer screamed.

"It's the ghost of Houdini!" I yelled.

"It's what's left of his corpse!" Johnny cried out.

Nat started to laugh, but the sounds choked in his throat.

The thing came closer into the red light. It was wet, and slimy, with pieces of skin dripping from it. It was small, like what was left of a body that had been buried for many years. It started to stand, its mouth beginning to open, slabs of flesh peeling from its chin.

Liz and Jennifer began to scream as dripping, slimy hands lifted into the air toward Nat. Only then did I see the hands were yellow. That they might actually be dishwashing gloves—my mother's

gloves!—coated with cold cream and grease. They reached out and touched Nat's hand. In a moment there was only one person screaming louder than everybody. It was Nat! He fell over backward in the chair, and as he did a yellowish, rusty coin flashed and fell with a CLINK from his pants pocket. It rolled across the floor as I heard a very familiar sound of *giggling*.

"Holy cow!" I whispered. "That's no ghost—it's Giggles!"

▶THIRTEEN◀

High Spirits!

I managed to get **Giggles** out of the lunchroom and cleaned up. Jennifer helped me.

"*I was a good mummy, right, Davie? Was I a good toilet-paper mummy? Davie? Davie?*"

"Yes, Giggles," I told her. "You were a very good mummy!"

I knew everyone in the Wacky Facts Lunch Bunch would agree. Without Giggles, Nat wouldn't have screamed and Mrs. Wilmont wouldn't have found out what a big crook he was, because none of us are squealers and we couldn't prove Nat had taken it. The Stonehenge coin was back and would be a prize, I hoped, for Liz.

I brought Giggles back to her classroom. I promised to buy her a present and take her trick

or treating for an extra hour. By the time I got back to Mrs. Wilmont's class everybody was busy having fun and talking about how great the Fright Party had been. Nat and Rado were the only ones who looked bad—especially Nat looked *really* scared now.

"Mrs. Wilmont told Nat to stay after school," Liz whispered to catch me up. "I'm sure she's going to give him a good lecture on how crime doesn't pay!"

"I hope she locks him up in a crypt and throws away the key," I said.

"WEEEEEEEEEEEEEEEEEEE!" Mrs. Wilmont blew her whistle for attention. This time it took a long time for everyone to quiet down.

"I've picked the winner of the talisman contest," she announced. "I want to award the Stonehenge coin before the other classes come to our room to see our work."

"If Liz McGinn won I'm going to puke," Nat mumbled.

"Me, too," Rado squeaked.

"I'd keep my thoughts to myself, Nat," Mrs. Wilmont warned.

Liz McGinn did win. Mrs. Wilmont motioned for Liz to come up to the front of the class, and handed her the coin. Before taking the coin Liz lifted the sparkling Dream Catcher high into the air. The an-

gel and cherub hands looked like they were reaching for the sky.

The Wacky Facts Lunch Bunch stood up in our robes, cheering and jumping up and down.

"WEEEEEEEEEEEEEEEEEEEEEE!" Mrs. Wilmont called for order again. "I want you all to understand why in my judgment Liz should be the winner of our talisman competition."

"Yeah, I'd like to know," Nat growled.

Mrs. Wilmont looked straight at Nat. "You might have won, Nat, because you did a great job making your project. I wish you'd work this hard more often. But you took the coin, so you shouldn't win it now. Besides, your charm is *second* best to Liz's. Your *devil's face* was inventively made, and if you use your creative talents as well in the future, I'm sure you will end up being a winner in school and in life."

Nat squirmed and turned rosy with everyone looking at him. In a second he was back to his usual rotten self. "I still don't understand why you think Liz's dumb piece of junk is better than mine. Can you tell me that?"

"I will tell you why," Mrs. Wilmont said. "I think Liz's Dream Catcher is more original. Besides, someday you'll understand that in this world, it's much more difficult to make an angel than a devil."

"Angels are big-time losers," Nat muttered.

"Not this time." Liz smiled heavenward as she held up her magic coin right in his face.

"Right on," I said, and the Wacky Facts Lunch Bunch cheered together, "Right on!"

Attack of the Killer Fishsticks

Team up with Action Dave and the Wacky Facts Lunch Bunch for their first mind-boggling adventure!

My name is Dave Martin and I'm president of the WACKY FACTS LUNCH BUNCH. My three best friends and I formed our club on the first day of school. Just like in most schools, the kids split up into different groups in the lunchroom. Liz, Johnny, Jennifer, and I don't fit into the Stuck-ups, the Brains, the Supernerds, the Zombies, or the Jocks. And we certainly weren't going to sit with the Nasty Blobs. The Nasty Blobs is our code name for Nat Bronski and Rado Clapp—the two most rotten, creepy, mean goons in our fifth grade class. They may be only two kids, but they are bonkers enough for a whole nuthouse.

Fifth Grade Safari

Join the Wacky Facts Lunch Bunch as they head out on a wild and freaky fifth grade safari!

It was the first time any of us in the WACKY FACTS LUNCH BUNCH had been to the zoo since it had been re-structured and made into a whole fantastic habitat.

"There aren't any more cages!" Jennifer said. "I'm glad about that. I used to think it was mean to put animals in prison."

"Me too," Max said. "Now they have moats and log fences and vines."

"Everything's so natural," I agreed. "It's like we're on safari in a real jungle!"

"The monkeys really look happy!" Johnny said, making goofy faces and grunting sounds at them.

"They think you're bonkers," Jennifer moaned, turning the camcorder on a couple of baboons who swung from branches and screeched.

"They're so cute," Liz said.

"*They're gross,*" a voice suddenly growled. It was Nat. The Nasty Blobs had followed us. They always try to stick their noses into anything we do.

"*All monkeys do is pick nits off each other,*" Nat babbled on.

"They do not," Liz defended them. "What do you know anyway?"

"They *love* nits," Rado squeaked.

We all turned to take a closer look at the monkeys. A lot of them *were* picking things off one another's heads.

"Monkeys just *groom* each other," I explained. "I read that in a *National Geographic* magazine."

"Yeah, Dave, I figured you'd know all about nits. Isn't that monkey on the left your cousin?" Nat howled.

"Buzz off," I told him.

The GROSS-OUT Lunch Contest!

Don't miss it!

Read **Fifth Grade Safari** for details.